W9-AFR-768

# FIREFLY SUMMER

## PURA BELPRÉ

PIÑATA
BOOKS

PIÑATA BOOKS
HOUSTON, TEXAS
1996

This volume is made possible through grants from the Rocke-feller Foundation, the National Endowment for the Arts (a federal agency), the Andrew W. Mellon Foundation, and the Lila Wallace-Reader's Digest Fund.

*Piñata Books are full of surprises!*

Piñata Books
A Division of Arte Público Press
University of Houston
Houston, Texas 77204-2174

Cover illustration and design by Kath Christensen

Belpré, Pura,
    Firefly summer / by Pura Belpré.
        p.    cm.
    Summary: At a plantation in rural Puerto Rico around the turn of the century the foreman pursues the mystery surrounding his family.
    ISBN 1-55885-174-7 (clothbound : alk. paper). —
    ISBN 1-55885-180-1 (pbk. : alk. paper)
    [1. Puerto Rico—Fiction.] I. Title.
PZ7.B4196F1    1996
[Fic]—dc20                                      96-15679
                                                    CIP
                                                     AC

The paper used in this publication meets the requirements of the American National Standard for Permanence of Paper for Printed Library Materials Z39.48-1984.

    1 2 3 4 5 6 7 8 9 0         10 9 8 7 6 5 4 3 2

*For Lala*

*She came that summer, and her laughter was to Grandmother as bright and merry as the dance of the fireflies on a dark night....*

# CONTENTS

CHAPTER

# FIREFLY SUMMER

# CHAPTER 1
# TERESA

It was recess time, and the front yard of the Baldorioty Grammar School in San Juan, Puerto Rico, was filled with a boisterous crowd of children, laughing and punching one another in an effort to get a glimpse of two lists of names posted on the bulletin board.

Teresa pushed through the group, elbowing her way until she reached the front. She could see the lists plainly now: one for the seventh and the other for the eighth grade, both representing the names of students who because of unusual school work during the year had been exempt from final examinations. She had waited for this opportunity, wishing and hoping she would make the list. Today she wanted it more than ever, for in her pocket was a letter from her grandmother, and the news it bore made her wish she were at home with her once more. Someone gave her a push which almost unbalanced her. She shot a fierce look at the two offenders who, standing on their toes, were scanning the lists, unaware of anybody else in the group. "Eighth graders," she said to herself, "the same pair who think they own the school." She regained her position and began to read the seventh-grade list. It had two rows of names. The first row was made mostly of boys' names. Her eyes followed the second row. She recognized many of the names: Milagros Santos, Eugenia Urrutia, María Hostos, Isabel Campos, and then her heart gave a jump which made her shut and open her eyes. There, between Fausto Milán and Rey Pino, was her name: Teresa Rodrigo. She looked at it intently, afraid she had made a mistake. The name was written so small, that it almost seemed like an afterthought. But it was real, her name was up, and the news in Grandmother's letter suddenly took on a new meaning. What difference did it make now if her uncle and aunt were away for two weeks and could not take her home? She would not stay in San Juan even if she had to go home alone. Relieved and happy, she turned to face the pushing crowd of children again. There was a solid barricade of them now, for the youngest ones, who had brothers or sisters or even first and second cousins in the school, had come to see if any of them had made the lists. She was tossed like a rubber ball every time she made an effort to break the line. The children shouted and laughed and held their ground with every fresh start she made. But she was determined to go through, and that she finally did. She rushed towards the great stairway that led up to Luna Street. Across from it was her aunt's home, where she lived when attending the city school.

"Teresa! Wait Teresa!" Six girls overtook her in the middle of the stairs.

"Come with us," said Angelina. "There is a large ship in the harbor. It came all the way from South America, and they are letting visitors in. It's sailing back late tonight. We're going to visit it after school."

Teresa shook her head and continued to climb the stairs.

"Oh, come along," said Mercedes, her chum and constant companion after school hours. "You have nothing else to do."

"I am not interested," said Teresa, "and I do have something else to do. Didn't you see my name in the list of exemptions, Mercedes? That means no more school for me. I'm on my way home."

"Home? This is only recess time," said Angelina.

"For you sixth graders," said Teresa. She ran up the rest of the way, leaving the girls wondering about her behavior. Even Mercedes was surprised and could not make her out. It was not like Teresa to miss a trip to the bay.

Teresa stopped at the entrance hall and re-read her grandmother's letter. It reassured her confidence. But what would Juana say when she heard of her new plan? She folded up the letter and climbed to the second floor where she lived.

Teresa's real home was a *finca* in the highlands, between Cayey and Cidra. There she lived with her parents and a maternal grandmother, besides Ramón, the boy who had come to live with them when he was six-years old and she only three. She was tall for her thirteen and one half years, with brown eyes that flashed at the least cause of excitement and a mop of thick black hair, which she wore in two braids tied together in the back with ribbons.

She tried the wrought-iron gate and found it locked. "Juana must be in the kitchen on the other side of the house," she thought.

"Juana! Juana!" she called, rattling the gate. She could hear her now, her heels clicking on the floor. Juana was her aunt's housekeeper, cook, maid and dressmaker all rolled into one. Her authority in the house was never disputed; it was as good as law. No one knew that better than she did, for both her Aunt Elvira and her Uncle Emilio had made it quite clear when she had first come to attend school in San Juan.

"What are you doing here so early?" asked Juana, as she struggled to open the gate.

Teresa did not answer, but followed her to the kitchen, where she had been preparing the noonday meal. She watched her cut a lemon and squeeze the juice into a glass, then fill the glass with water and sweeten it.

"It is rather early for your drink," she said, handing her the glass, "but you might as well have it. Perhaps you will tell me what all this means."

"Oh, Juana, I've made the exemption list, and I'm going home," Teresa said joyfully.

"Home? How can you go when school is still going on?"

"But you don't understand. I don't have to stay until the end of the term now. I don't have to take final exams."

"That doesn't mean anything," said Juana, "especially when your aunt is away. There is no one to take you home."

Teresa pushed the glass of lemonade away. She had to make Juana understand how important it was for her to leave for home immediately. She took the letter out of her pocket and read it to her.

"The Feast of the Cross!" said Juana. "Well, that is something worth going home to."

"Will you let me go then?" She waited for an answer, which did not come.

Juana had gone back to her work and apparently had forgotten all, even Teresa. But actually she had not. Her mind was now filled with the picture of the Feast as she had known it, and a longing to enjoy it again rose within her. As she worked she made her decision. She could take Teresa home and...yes, that was it; she, too, would enjoy the Feast of the Cross. She glanced at Teresa, who sat quietly looking at her drink.

Teresa, too, had been planning, only her plans did not include Juana. She had enough money in her trunk, and there were coaches in San Juan you could hire. She would go home even if she had to go alone. She pushed the stool under the table and began to leave the kitchen.

"Wait, Teresa," said Juana. "Since you are not going back to school, stay here while I go out for a while."

She took off her apron and hung it on the peg on the wall and, with no more explanation, headed for the stairs.

Teresa ran to the balcony in time to see Juana reach the street. She watched her walk to the end and turn towards the public plaza, the square in the center of the city.

Across the street, the school yard was deserted. Teresa wondered what the teacher had said when she failed to return to class. What if she crossed her name off the list and sent home for her? She dismissed the idea from her mind and returned to the kitchen to wait for Juana. The lemonade tasted better now after having set for a while. She hoped Juana had not gone shopping. If she had, it would be hours before she returned. Juana did more bargaining than buying. She had seen her bargain with the vegetable man at the foot of the stairs, with the grocery man on the corner, even with the charcoal man. *"Cielos,"* she said, "don't let her be shopping."

But Juana was not shopping, as Teresa feared, but trying to hire a coach to take them to the *finca.* She stood in the middle of the plaza, looking over the number of coaches that stood around. At last she saw one which was being shined. There was a group of men around the driver. "Filimón, the very man I want to see."

*"Buenos tardes,* Filimón," she said. "Your coach is shinier than a mirror, and well might it be, for tomorrow it will take Don Rodrigo's daughter home."

*"Señora,"* said a man at her side, "I have been here for hours. You can't put in your order before I do."

"Nor before I do either," said another. "I need this coach. I will pay you a little more, Filimón, if you let me have it. What do you say, *hombre?"*

If Filimón had been bitten by a tarantula, he would not have jumped quicker.

"What do I say?" he roared. "You dare bribe me, *monsieur!"*

Then followed a harangue of French patois, which was lost on his listeners. Filimón came from Martinique, and when he lost his temper, he forgot the Spanish he had learned in Puerto Rico.

"But, Filimón," pleaded the customers.

"*C'est tout...y basta*," he said, going back to his work.

The group dispersed. Some went back to the other coaches and tried to hire them, although they knew they were inferior and the drivers less careful. All left, except Juana. She did not come to the plaza to have Filimón turn her back because of a fit of temper. Her fifty years had taught her how to cope with tempers.

"Filimón," she said, approaching him, "I have come to hire your coach and no other. Don Rodrigo's daughter must get home tomorrow. She must be at the *finca* in time for the Feast of the Cross."

Juana never quite knew what did it. When Filimón turned to face her, he was a changed man.

"Ah!" he said, smiling, "the Feast of the Cross *est une belle ocasion*."

Juana noticed the change and made the best of it, explaining how Teresa had missed it the year before.

"*Pobrecita*," said Filimón. "She will not miss it again."

"I, Filimón, will hire you this coach and I will drive it myself."

"*Gracias*," said Juana. "Come early tomorrow morning to 67 Luna Street."

"*Oui, madame*, tomorrow." He went back to his coach and gave it an extra rub.

"*Mon Dieux*," he said aloud, "the Feast of the Cross...*Comme est belle!*"

# CHAPTER 2
# THE TRIP TO THE *FINCA*

For the first time since Teresa had been coming to the city school, Juana did not have to wake her. She was up and ready by six o'clock, delighted over the fact that Juana was going home with her. She wrote three letters: one for her aunt, which she left on her desk, one for her teacher and another for Mercedes. The last two she tied on the bolt of the gate, where she was sure Mercedes would find them that afternoon when she came calling.

Juana sent her to her friend Doña Josefa, across the street, to ask if she would take care of the canary and water the plants in the gallery while she was gone. When she returned from her errand, the coach was at the door, and Filimón was bringing her trunk down. Juana followed with her hands full of extra packages.

"Here I am, petite," he said, laughing. "Filimón always keeps his word."

"And I will pray for a special favor for you," said Teresa, climbing to her seat in the rear of the coach.

From there she reminded Juana that Doña Josefa wanted the house key, otherwise how was she to get in the house? She took the extra packages, fixed them on the rest of the seat and waited for Juana to come back. "I hope she will sit in the front with Filimón," she said to herself. Her wish was granted: Juana returned, took a look at the packages in the rear of the coach and decided on the front seat.

Filimón picked up the reins and started the coach. It rattled over the cobbled street. The clatter of the horse's hooves brought a group of sleepy-eyed children to their doors. On the corner of Cruz Street, the coach turned and rode down to Fortaleza. Teresa shot a quick glance at the Governor's Palace at the head of the street. Only a month ago, she had been taken to see the strange flowers that grew there. She had made a picture of a beautiful orchid and given it to Doña Clara. She had been so pleased with it that she had promised to take her again when she went calling. Doña Clara had been going to the Governor's castle for years to paint pictures of the garden, many of which now hung on the castle's walls.

They went past the Plaza Cristobal Colón, where the statute of the discoverer stood high on a pedestal overlooking the Municipal Theatre and the San Cristóbal Fort. They continued out towards Puerta de Tierra. Teresa hoped Mercedes had come with her instead of having to stay in the city. Mercedes had no mother. She lived with Lucio, her father, and her old cousin Flora.

When they reached Santurce, the coach had to stop at an intersection to let the trolley car pass by on its way to the Condado, the rich suburb by the sea. The few passengers waved, and Teresa waved back. The traffic was beginning to crowd the street, and Filimón had to drive slower than he really wanted. When finally they were again on the road, he sent his horses flying. The packages tumbled out of the seat and Teresa had to pick them up while holding on to the sides of the coach for balance. They were soon in Río Piedras and passing in front of the University of Puerto Rico. There were students at the campus, and Teresa thought of her friend Sixta who was studying to be a teacher. Sixta lived across the road from the *finca*, and though she was nineteen-years old, she was one of Teresa's best friends. "Someday, I will be going there, too," thought Teresa. "Someday there will be enough schools for all the children of the *fincas*. I would rather teach at a *finca* than anywhere else." She had not told her plans to her family yet, only to Sixta, who also shared her dream. "Maybe I will get Juanita to do the same, and Angelina and even Fausto. Their fathers own *fincas* and can send them to the city school. But there are all those children of the workers," she thought, "who could not afford to come, and the few schools available are miles away."

They left Río Piedras, and now the entire countryside unfolded like a great panorama before their eyes. This was the country, with is long stretches of beautiful green fields, deep, deep valleys and mountains that rose like chains of emeralds topped with lavender, purple, and yellow. Now and then from different sections of the land they were crossing rose clusters of bamboo, which resembled sugar cane. Teresa looked out of the coach at a large tree which topped all others. It was a ceiba, like the ones on the road that led to her *finca*. They were sturdy trees from which furniture was made.

The coach was approaching fruit groves. There were trees laden heavily with large grapefruits and pineapples growing on the spaces between the trees. The sight brought to her mind the picture of the *finca* at her home, though it was not a fruit farm, like the one they were approaching, but a tobacco plantation. Yet on the outskirts of the *finca*, during the summer the workers planted vegetables, fruits and other crops for home consumption. The *finca*! How she missed it! Gone were the hours she spent watching the preparations for the planting of tobacco, but clear in her mind was the picture of the cool foothills, mountain slopes with carefully laid out plots. She envisioned the farm workers bending over the first tobacco shoots, so precious to her father, tending them until they were ready for transplanting. She remembered the first time she had seen the first plots covered with cheesecloth to protect the shoots. At first she had not known what they were, looking to her like clouds dropped from the sky. "Come and see the clouds," her father always said, whenever the workers were busy covering the patches.

They were close to the fruit farm now. The laborers had baskets filled with fruit strapped to their backs. One of the youngest of the workers came to the edge of the road to look at the coach. He had a band across his forehead to keep his hair out of his eyes and to sop up the perspiration. His resemblance to Ramón made her jump to the side of the coach, from where she could take a better look at him. He was strong, tall and brown-skinned, with high cheekbones and small eyes. He could easily pass for Ramón's twin brother. "Poor Ramón," she said aloud.

"Did you say something?" asked Juana, turning back.

"Oh, no," she answered quickly. Here she was thinking aloud again. Yet, that boy at that farm did look like Ramón. She must not forget to tell him when she reached home.

Juana and Filimón were engaged in conversation, and now and then parts of sentences came back to her above the noise of the wheels on the road. Filimón was telling Juana how he had come to own a line of coaches in San Juan. He had two horses in a stable in Caguas, which he would exchange for the ones pulling the coach now. "Fresh ones for the remainder of the trip," she heard him explain.

All along the road to Caguas the *flamboyán* trees were ready to bloom. Teresa wished she could have made the trip two weeks later. Then she would have seen them shining bright red as if ablaze. There was one *flamboyán* tree along the road to Cidra which she and Sixta saw one summer when it burst into flowers. She had never forgotten the sight of it. Later on in the year, they had stood under its branches to listen to the "Housewives tales," as they called the murmuring sound of the dry long pods that come out after the blooms fell. Grandmother had told her many of the legends connected with the tree. She often thought of the girl who stood under it every year, waiting for the blooms to open and having her wish come true.

When they entered Caguas, Filimón rode to the outskirts of the town to exchange his team of horses. How fast the coach went now. Soon they were out in the middle of the road again and nearing a small store on the side of a hill. The sound of children's voices reached their ears.

"Where are they, Juana? Can you see them from your seat?" Teresa cried excitedly.

"There, under the trees, petite," said Filimón, stopping the coach.

At the sight of the coach, the children scampered from under the trees, shouting, "Compre... compre flores—Buy, buy flowers." Their hands were full of bunches of wild flowers wrapped in green leaves. Juana bought two bunches and gave them to Teresa, then went into the store. Teresa stayed with the children at the edge of the hill, from where they tried to point to their homes for her. One little girl gave Teresa a bunch of wild strawberries she had picked along the road.

"Come inside and see what you want, Teresa," called Juana.

The store was one large room with a counter stretching the full length. On it were bottles of soft drinks, homemade candy and baskets of freshly made cheese. Bunches of ripe bananas hung from the rafters, and the floor was filled with sacks of brown sugar, rice, coffee and a variety of beans.

"I want some cheese and crackers," said Teresa. She picked up two boxes of crackers. "For the children," she told Juana. "Why don't you buy them something, too?"

Juana gave her a handful of coconut candy. Teresa divided the crackers and candy among the children who were sitting on the side of the road. It was nice to sit there with them, eating and looking far down the hill at the thatched houses on stilts.

Filimón came out of the store drinking a bottle of tamarind juice and smacking his lips at its tartness. He leaned against the door, gurgling and making faces with each swallow. When he finished, he took his seat on the coach again. That was his signal for them to follow. The children jumped out of the way.

"Goodbye!" they called as the coach rode away.

Refreshed now, Teresa settled in her seat comfortably. It felt good to have left the coach for a while. Filimón was driving faster now, and Teresa thought he deserved to be called the best driver in the land. He knew every turn and curve of the road.

As the coach turned, they came within view of a white house on a hill. It was the largest one she had seen since leaving Caguas. The sloping ground and the cluster of shrubs surrounding it reminded her of her own home. She wondered if that house had a long passageway connecting the front and rear of the house, like her home. She had begun to call the passageway a "neck" when she was a child, and since then no one in the house called it by any other name. She looked back at the house as the coach went by and noticed that the house was square on the back and had an open balcony with potted plants everywhere. She was glad it did not have a "neck."

The brown and white house she lived in was an old house, where two generations of Rodrigos had lived and tilled the soil they owned. For Teresa, the nicest and most livable part of it was the "neck." It was there where her grandmother kept her rare plants, her mother her sewing basket, and her father his desk full of catalogs from which he and Ramón made their orders. It had two windows from which one could see the entire countryside. There were two rocking chairs, from where her grandmother's cat, Filo, and Ramón's old dog, Leal, were constantly being pushed off. The oldest possession in the neck was a rose-colored conch shell that stood on a table made of empty spools of thread, painted the colors of the rainbow. The conch shell was used as a horn to signal the time of day for the *finca* workers. At noon, it heralded the arrival of the wives and daughters with their frugal meal, and at six o'clock it told them the working day was over. Sometimes, when there were unusual events at the *finca*, the conch shell sent out a special blast over the hills. Every year Teresa had tried unsuccessfully to blow sound out of the shell, but had to be content instead to listen to the sound of the sea by putting it close to her ears. Her lungs were not strong enough to make the shell vibrate its mournful call.

Teresa wondered if any of the workers had left the *finca* while she was away at school. She was always meeting new additions upon her return home. Would José still be there? José, the dreamer, who thought nothing of spending all his pay when friends came to see him from Cayey. José, who dreamed of the day when all the workers would own enough land to be their own masters.

Then there was Gregorio. He was a laborer with political ideas, always eager to know the latest news, although he did not know how to read. How many times during the summer months had she helped his three daughters read aloud to him, and how she had admired the way he interpreted the news to the other workers at the *finca*. He had even promised to marry his daughters to politicians. She wondered if he had found any suitors available for his Lola, Ernestina and Panchita? Teresa would have to ask her grandmother about that.

Whatever changes she might find at the *finca*, she was glad they would not include Felipe, the overseer, and his wife Pilar. Nor Lucía, who came daily to help her mother. Nor Antonio, Lucía's eight-year-old son who ran in and out of the house all day long. It was good to come home and know that Sixta's family was across the road down the hill. Teresa would again spend days sitting under the trees, watching Sixta do her drawn work for the stores in the town and listening to her tales about the university.

There was one neighbor whom she would rather not see: Don Gumersindo Vázquez. Teresa hoped he was gone. He was the miser of all the *fincas* in the district. No one liked how he used his three daughters in the fields. They did twice the work of any laborer. No one ever saw them outside the fields. Teresa often wondered if they had ever gone back to Cayey since the burial of their mother. No, she did not like Don Gumersindo Vázquez.

"Look out back there," cried Filimón.

The coach rocked, sending all the packages to the floor. Teresa held fast to the sides of the coach. The road was filled with prisoners cutting stones, leaving very little clear space to ride on. Filimón broke into one of his long harangues of Patois and Spanish which was impossible to understand. The coach swerved, and he kept a tight hold on the reins. The pile of cut stones extended as far as the eye could see. Teresa wished Filimón would let them walk rather than stay in the coach, jolting as it was. Finally, after much rattling of wheels and clattering of hooves, they were again on the clear side of the road. Teresa picked up the packages and arranged them on the seat beside her. The box of color paints she was bringing for Ramón was torn, and she had to hold it on her lap for fear the small bottles would roll on the floor again and break. She knew how much Ramón had wanted a real box of paints, and at last she had been able to get it for him.

Besides the *finca* and the horses, there was nothing Ramón liked better than paints, which he used for decorating most of the simple carvings he did about the *finca*. He decorated wooden spoons and forks with pictures of palms and butterflies for display on the little tables in the parlor. He also painted scenes on *güiros* made out of gourds, to be played by peasants in their native orchestras. She called them scratchers, for they were grooved and the noise they made came out by scratching a wire fork across them. There were güiros of all shapes and sizes all over the house.

Teresa often wondered what would have become of Ramón if he had not come to live at the *finca*. She remembered how surprised Mercedes had been when Teresa first told her his story. It all had happened when she had asked if Ramón was her brother, and she had said yes and no. She could still remember the look that came over Mercedes' face. Then Teresa told her the story from the very beginning. How her father, Don Rodrigo, had gone to a *finca* near Guayama to buy some shares in a sugar refinery and had seen Ramón among a group of children who had come to beg to mind his horse. While the rest of the children jumped and shouted, Ramón stood quietly, hands stretched towards the horse, but not daring to touch it. He kept saying "caballo mío, caballo mío—my horse, my horse."

Ramón had followed Teresa's father around the plant and even waited outside the office for him. Every time Don Rodrigo went to the plant, the same thing had happened, until her father finally made inquiries and found out that Ramón was an orphan who lived with a laborer who had six other children of his own. He learned that Ramón's parents had been victims of a hurricane. So, on the last visit to the refinery, her father had asked the laborer for Ramón. So earnest was his plea that he was able to adopt Ramón. Ramón arrived at the *finca* holding a carton box with his few clothes and a small sandalwood box wrapped in layers of old newspapers. When it was opened, they found a coral necklace and a pair of earrings that matched it.

"And he has been at the *finca* ever since?" Mercedes had asked.

It was a silly question to ask, but she was always asking silly questions, like a small child. Ever since Teresa had told her that Ramón had given her the sandalwood box as a birthday present when she was eleven-years old, Mercedes had wanted her to bring it to San Juan so that she could see it. Every year Teresa disappointed her, for she had the box in the bottom of her old trunk, wrapped up in one of her father's large handkerchieves. Ramón believed the necklace had belonged to his mother, and now that it had come to be Teresa's, she wanted to keep it as safe as he had himself. Finally, she had compromised with Mercedes by promising to show it to her if she ever came to visit her *finca*.

Teresa had been so absorbed in her thoughts that she did not notice how far they had ridden. The road looked extremely familiar. There was the old farmhouse which had been burned almost to the ground the summer before. It was still abandoned. The coach was turning, leaving the main road behind and entering the bumpy country road that led to the *finca*.

"There go the packages again," she said as the coach jolted. Teresa made no effort to pick them up from under the seat where they had rolled, because already way up on the hill the roof of the white and brown house had come into view.

"Juana," she cried, "look, up there is home. We have arrived at the *finca*."

# CHAPTER 3
# THE FEAST OF THE CROSS

Teresa's unexpected arrival was cause for great excitement. Her grandmother, who was working in her garden on the south side of the house, saw her alight from the coach and run up the path.

"Rodrigo! Anita! Ramón!" she called. "Teresa has come home."

Before any of them had come to her call, Teresa reached her grandmother. Leal, disturbed from his nap, came out of the house barking and growling. At the sight of Teresa he jumped on her, licking her hands and face. "Down, Leal, down," she said, but Leal kept up his welcome until Ramón called him.

"Aquí, Leal, aquí," he said softly, and Leal went back to his master and settled down at his feet.

No one noticed Juana coming up the hill until she stood close to them.

"Why, Juana," said Doña Anita, "what are you doing here? Has anything happened to Emilio?"

"No, Doña Anita," she answered. "The family is away. Someone had to bring Teresa home. There has been little peace in the house ever since her grandmother's letter arrived."

"But school is not closed yet. How did you manage that?"

"I did not have to," said Teresa proudly. "I made the list."

"And what does making a list mean," asked her father.

"That I did not have to stay for examinations. So what was the use of staying any longer in San Juan, when the feast of the Cross was coming along? Has it begun, Ramón?"

"Not yet, Teresa. I am going to build a new shed for it this year."

Ramón was glad she was home. Last year the feast did not seem the same to him with Teresa in San Juan.

"I brought you a box of paints," she said. "Filimón will bring it up with the rest of the packages."

When Filimón brought the trunk and the packages up, the family went back to the house.

Everything looked the same way, and Teresa took in all her familiar nooks and corners, glad to be back home once more.

Her parents also looked the same. But Ramón had changed. He already looked as tall as her father, and her father was the tallest man at the *finca*.

The three men began to talk about the trip, when something her father said made Filimón laugh loud and hardy.

Don Rodrigo was a good-natured man, with a strong body, as sturdy as some of the old trees in his *finca*. His eyes were brown and lively, like his daughter's, and he had abundant hair which the sun had tinted the shade of an early autumn leaf. He cultivated a moustache which covered his upper lip and added maturity to his face. But Don Rodrigo was only fifty, an age which made him remark that half of his existence had been spread over the hills of his *finca*.

Before Filimón left, Teresa's grandmother gave him a cup of steaming black coffee. He stood outside the door, talking and laughing, waiting for the coffee to cool.

Grandmother was the practical member of the family. She knew how to please everyone who came to the house, no matter who he was. Her snow-white hair contrasted with the firmness of her face, and her energy made her daughter seem like an invalid around the house.

Regardless of Grandmother's age, she and her daughter looked much alike. Both had angular faces, thin sharp noses and exactly the same color of almond-shaped eyes: a pale-bluish color, which Grandmother said had been her father's legacy.

Grandmother's parents, like the Rodrigo's, had been country people, living away from the excitement of towns and cities. They loved the land and the serenity of the hills which surrounded them.

With Teresa now in the house, plans for the feast began in earnest. The feast, so eagerly awaited by all, was a floral celebration in honor of the Cross, similar in character to the feasts of the Cross of May held in various provinces in Spain, from where the custom found its tradition. It had been well implanted in Puerto Rico, especially in the towns and countryside.

To celebrate it, nine rosaries were chanted on an improvised altar, for which nine movable steps were made. One step was added each night to show the progress of the feast. Nine godfathers or godmothers, whose duties were to dress the altar and lead the rosary, were selected by the hostess. To set them apart from the rest of the crowd attending the feast, a small white bow was pinned on their chests.

News of the approaching feast soon reached every worker on the *finca*. The air of gaiety mounted in each house as the days went on. Housewives began to alter old blouses and skirts, adding a ribbon or a ruffle in their efforts to have something new to wear at the feast. Even the children did not escape the excitement. They, too, took things in their own hands. The older ones renewed their efforts to help more around the house, and the younger ones managed to keep out of mischief, afraid to be deprived of the privilege of attending the festivities.

One day, late in the afternoon, Gregorio and José climbed the hill to see Ramón and Valentín, who were in charge of building the new shed for the altar.

"I wonder how the feast day will go this year?" said José.

"You fared well last summer," Gregorio said. "Where did you learn to sing those carols?"

"That's the way they sing them in Ponce. I learned them long ago when I used to work there."

"Hm," said Gregorio, pulling at his cigar, "that is about the only thing that scares me about the ceremonies. I can't whistle a tune."

When they reached the shed, they found that Ramón was laying down the floor.

"I don't see why they have taken so long to build this shed," said José. "The walls are not even up yet."

"When do you figure the walls will be done, Ramón?" they asked.

"There won't be any," Ramón answered.

"No walls? Why?"

"To let everyone who can't get seats inside see the altar from the outside. They can sit on the grass, provided it doesn't rain."

"A good idea," they said, remembering how many times last summer they had to wait to see the altar after the crowd had left the shed.

They waited for Valentín to put away the tools and then walked down the hill together, discussing previous celebrations.

Little by little the work progressed, and then came the day when at last the shed was finished, with its new altar and nine steps. Ramón bought three lanterns to hang on the ceiling. Word was sent to the workers that Wednesday the feast would begin.

The day before the opening, Grandmother asked her daughter about the list of godmothers and godfathers for the feast.

"Let's not make it beforehand, *Mamá*. It will be more fun to select them from the group that comes each night."

"But we have to have someone in charge the first night," said Grandmother.

"What about you, *Mamá*? How would you like to wear the first ribbon?"

"Why I have not sung a feast since I was a young woman, but I believe I would like to do it again."

"Very well, then you shall be the first godmother," said her daughter.

Grandmother was more excited than she cared to confess.

"We have to make the "capias," ribbons, and the altar must be dressed, and the refreshments selected," she said, growing more and more excited.

Teresa came into the room at that moment, and an idea came to her: Teresa was old enough to take some of the responsibility of the feast, especially when one of the family was involved.

"I am to be the first godmother, Teresa," she said. "How would you like to make the *capias* for the feast?"

"Oh, Grandmother, do you really mean it? Make all the *capias*? There's nothing I would like better," she said.

"Then get Antonio to fasten the safety pins on for you."

While Teresa ran to the kitchen to tell Antonio the news, her grandmother brought the work basket and took out a roll of narrow white ribbon, thread, needles, and a carton of small safety pins.

"Let's go to the neck to work," said Teresa, gathering up her work.

"Did Grandmother ask to be the first godmother?" asked Antonio, putting up his forefingers so that Teresa could wind the ribbon around them. Teresa wanted the *capias* to be real butterfly bows.

"No, no, Mother selected her, of course."

"But do you suppose she wished for it beforehand?"

"Now, Antonio, who could possibly know that? Don't wiggle your fingers. I don't want these *capias* to be loose."

"Who else will get *capias* this summer, Teresa?"

"I don't know that either," she answered.

When Teresa had finished making the *capias*, she asked Antonio to begin attaching the safety pins while she went to look for an empty box to put the bows in.

No sooner was she gone than Antonio pinned a *capia* to his shirt. He smoothed the ribbon gently. "I wish I was big enough to get one of these *capias*," he said, unfastening the safety pin. When he finished his work, the nine *capias* looked like small white butterflies with their wings wide open.

Teresa had not found a box, but she had a large piece of tissue paper. "This will have to do," she said. She wrapped the *capias* and went to the shed to find her grandmother.

"They are beautiful," said Grandmother, "but why didn't you sew them."

"Because they looked better tied like that, don't you think?"

"Yes, I do. Come now and give me a hand here."

They spread a white runner over the altar and put on the first step. Ramón brought the mahogany cross he had made for the feast and stood it on the altar. Antonio placed jugs at either side of it.

"That's all I want now, except for the flowers which I will cut tomorrow," said Grandmother.

"I must not forget to bring your chair, Grandmother," said Ramón. "I better bring it at once."

That night after dinner, Doña Anita assigned each member of the family a special job to do. Juana was to make the *manjar*—a dish made of milk, rice, flour and yolks of eggs, sweetened with sugar and sprinkled with cinnamon.

Lucía, Antonio's mother, was to help Teresa's grandmother with the tomato marmalade for the *casabe* bread. Teresa had to prepare the *sangría*—diluted wine with lemon, water and sugar. Ramón was to ride to Cayey and bring the cookies Lucía's husband had ordered from the baker. Lucía herself would brew the coffee for the men who she knew would pass up the *sangría*.

Next day by mid-afternoon, everything was ready.

A large table was brought out and placed at the kitchen entrance, and plates, spoons, cups and saucers were piled on it. Juana and Lucía were put in charge.

At sundown, the workers began to arrive, and the shed was soon filled. Those who could not find seats sat outside on the grass. There were eleven children, and Teresa and Ramón gave them the first bench, right next to her grandmother. "This will be your seat for the entire feast," Ramón said. The children were delighted.

"There are lots of new faces," said Teresa. "Do they live on our *finca*?"

"No," Ramón answered. "Have you forgotten how many guests come every year with the workers?"

When they were settled, Grandmother took the crystal beads off the altar and began her offering. "Oh, Holy Cross, we who gather here humbly offer you this floral feast of May," she said. Then she began to chant the rosary.

The workers all joined her enthusiastically. On and on she led them. When she reached the "Adórate—We adore thee," the workers took the leading choruses, singing with abandon and gaiety. There were all types of voices, and the merging of them, though somewhat dissonant, gave the feast the mark of spontaneity for which it was known. Grandmother followed with the "Salve Regina," which she sang alone in her thin but firm voice. After that, she closed with a carol for the Cross.

The workers applauded and thanked her for the way she had opened the feast. Those who had been sitting on the grass stood up to stretch their legs and light their cigars. But when Doña Anita stood up with the new *capia* in her hands, a great silence fell over the group. The children stood on their benches to see who would get the new *capia*. She went in and out of the line of benches as if she were looking for a special person. She left the shed and went out to a group of men who stood with José and pinned the *capia* on Gregorio's chest.

Poor Gregorio, taken by surprise, almost jumped out of his shoes.

"Say something, *hombre*," said his friends.

But Gregorio, known for his political speeches, now could not think of anything to say.

"*Vamos*, Gregorio," said José, "a *capia* is a *capia*, and you have to accept it. Can't you even do that?"

Gregorio bowed to Doña Anita and thanked her while the crowd shouted and applauded.

"Now," said Don Rodrigo, "let us all have refreshments and a toast to the new godfather of the feast."

Juana and Lucía served everyone, and the group spread about the place eating and drinking *sangría* and black coffee.

Teresa sat at the edge of the shed with the children, watching the stars between mouthfuls of *manjar*. Ramón kept running back and forth, bringing them extra portions of cookies and glasses of the *sangría*.

Finally, the workers began to leave, and the family walked to the edge of the hill with them.

The next day it was Gregorio's turn to honor the Cross.

At noon his wife, Fermina, came to dress the altar. She added a second step to mark the second rosary and stood the mahogany cross on it. Then she spread a blue runner with a heavy crochet border on the altar and asked Ramón for an extra chair. She refilled the jugs with fresh water and put in carnations she had brought.

Teresa and Ramón watched her work, wondering all the time why she had asked for the extra chair. But Fermina left without telling them the reason.

Late that afternoon, the family came out to the shed. Already a group of workers were sitting admiring the altar, and soon after they saw Gregorio's family coming up the hill. With them came Nicanor, the town guitarist, holding his guitar under his arm. They were followed by children, skipping and laughing.

"*Buenas tardes*," said Gregorio, taking his chair and offering Nicanor the other one.

Teresa and Ramón looked at each other. This was the reason for the extra chair. Gregorio was going to have music tonight. They were glad their seats were close enough so that they could watch Nicanor play.

The workers soon began to fill the shed, and again there was a surplus sitting out on the grass. Gregorio picked up the crystal beads and began the rosary. There were no frills to the simple way in which he conducted the prayer. When he finished, he nodded to Nicanor, who began to pluck his guitar. His tune rose tenderly and plaintively. On and on he played, and the crowd sat quietly listening. How long he played no one really knew. They sat absorbed in it, as if the strings of his guitar were magic threads that held them to their seats. Every eye was on the Cross, and every mind was filled with the solemnity of the moment. There were no carols sung in praise of the Cross, yet there was a carol in each of the hearts of those gathered there. When the music ceased, the group still sat quietly until Don Rodrigo broke the spell with loud applause. Everyone went up to Nicanor and thanked him for the music and also thanked Gregorio for having thought of it.

"Music was a splendid offering," said Grandmother. "Whatever made you decide upon it?"

"I can't sing," said Gregorio. "I had to have Nicanor do the singing for me. That, I think, he has done well."

The third *capia* went to one of the guests of the workers, a young woman from another *finca*.

"Play an extra tune," she asked Nicanor.

"One tune for Rosa, please," said Benito, who had brought her to the feast.

"If I do, who will sing?" asked Nicanor.

Then came a loud call for "Pilar, Pilar."

"Sing *La Borinqueña*," said Rosa.

"No, no," cried the children. "Sing *Flor de té* first."

They had never forgotten the plight of the shepherd boy who lost his shepherdess to a king. The song was as good as a story to them. "Sing it, please, Pilar," they pleaded.

So she sang it for them and then sang *La Borinqueña* for everybody else. Before she had gone very far, the entire crowd joined her in the song they all knew and loved. Inspired by it, Nicanor continued to play until the workers were ready to go home.

So the feast progressed night after night, one rivaling with the other in originality, until the time came when there were eight steps leading to the Cross. That evening, the *capia* had fallen to Sixta's mother. She had dressed the altar in bright red and had filled the earthen jugs with tall branches of red berries.

All morning the children had sat watching her work, dressing the altar as bright as the blossoms of the *flamboyán* tree.

The altar was covered by white muslin, on which rosebuds of red crepe paper had been pinned. The steps to the Cross were hidden by masses of rosebuds delicately fashioned.

"You must have sat all night making those rosebuds," said Doña Anita.

"Good work," said Grandmother. "I think, this is one of the prettiest altars I have ever seen here, María."

"I'm glad to be here to see it, too," said Teresa.

That night the crowd was as large as on the first night, for the eve of the last rosary meant a chance to close the feast, if the last *capia* was pinned on you. That was a thing many a worker wished for. When they had walked around the altar and had told María how much they admired her work, they went back to their benches, and María began the rosary.

When she finished and closed with two improvised carols, Doña Anita stood up with a small box in her hands, out of which she took three *capias*. A loud murmur rose from the crowd; Teresa and Antonio exchanged glances quickly. There were two extra *capias* in Doña Anita's hand, which they knew they had not made. Who, then, had made them? And why? They were not the only ones who wondered about them. The workers, too, were certain Doña Anita had made a mistake. Hadn't she noticed the eight steps on the altar? Had she forgotten how many *capias* had been given already?

But Doña Anita knew what she was doing. She crossed the shed and came to the bench where the children sat behind María and pinned one *capia* on Ramón, one on Antonio and the other on Teresa.

"The children! Three *capias* for children," cried the workers, shaking their heads in disapproval. This was the first time anything like that had happened. Why had she wasted three good *capias* on the children when the shed was full of grown people? True, Ramón was almost a man. Did they not take orders from him now and then in things concerning the *finca*? But there was Teresa, only eleven, and Antonio, who was just eight-years old. They did not know what to make of Doña Anita's choice.

But the children were delighted.

"*Gracias, gracias, Mamá*," said Teresa, kissing her.

"The closing of the feast," said Ramón, conscious of the honor Doña Anita had conferred upon them. "Oh, Doña Anita, I do not know what to say."

But Antonio said not a word. He stood in their midst looking at the butterfly bow on his chest. Teresa and Ramón had received the two extra *capias*, but he had the last of the ones he had helped make. Perhaps it was the very one he had pinned on his chest that day when Teresa had left him alone for just a minute…the very day he had wished to be grown up, so he too could have a chance at one of them. And here he was now with a *capia* on his chest and still a small boy. He looked at he rest of the children on the bench and smiled a smile of complete satisfaction and pride.

On the morning following the unusual events, Teresa and Ramón were up earlier than ever. When they came to the shed, they were surprised to find Antonio surrounded by a group of children.

"They want to help," he said.

"All right," said Teresa. "We are going to pick ferns, come along."

"I know a place that is not far, and it's full of young plants," said Roberto.

"Let's go there," said Ramón. "Lead us to it."

Roberto led them to a secluded spot near the spring, where the young ferns looked like plums and the green moss stretched out like a rug.

"Let's carry some of the moss, too," said Teresa. "Antonio, you and the boys stay here while Ramón and I cut some branches from these bushes. We'll need lots of them."

The place was full of wild violets and there was a row of hyacinths ready to blossom. While Ramón cut the branches, Teresa gathered the flowers and piled them near the moss the children had gathered. When they had a large pile of branches, ferns and flowers, Ramón, sorted them out and gave each their share to carry.

Once again at the shed, they settled to work. Ramón brought a ladder, and Antonio climbed up to place the last step on the altar. He stood the mahogany cross on it. Teresa handed him handfuls of ferns, which he began to spread on the steps until they were all covered. The rest of the children helped Teresa cover the altar with the moss and the remaining ferns until not a piece of wood was seen. Meanwhile, Ramón had stood the branches around the rear of the altar. He had even covered the ladder Antonio had climbed previously to make it look like a tree.

"The shed looks like a grotto, Ramón," said Teresa. "Do we have to have all three lanterns on tonight? I wish we could have just one over the cross."

"I can move two of them further back, but we have to have them all, even though the moon shines so clear." He brought the long ladder from the wood-shed and untied the two lanterns from the rafters where they had hung. He then tied them in the rear of the shed, leaving just the one over the cross.

When Doña Anita came to look at their work, she was surprised to see what they had accomplished. Grandmother, too, came bringing arms full of freshly cut flowers from her garden.

"It is simple and beautiful," she said.

"Do you think *Papá* will like it?" asked Teresa.

"I am sure he will," she answered.

They sat to watch the children sort the flowers and place some in the earthen jugs. The smaller ones went into the making of three bouquets and a tiny wreath. They wrapped them in long leaves and brought them to the house to keep them fresh for the evening.

"Now to start the carols," said Teresa. "We have to teach Antonio his, and drill him until he knows it by heart."

"May we stay, too?" asked the rest of the children.

"Carols are surprises," Teresa explained. "You will hear them tonight."

The children left, promising to come early and see if there was anything else they could do. Though they had not received *capias*, the other children felt part of the last day of the feast because their friend Antonio had one.

In the midst of drilling Antonio, Grandmother called Teresa. A peasant had come with a box for her. She ran to the kitchen. She did not know the man. The box was square and tied with a strong cord. On one side of it was a scrap of paper pasted with her name written on it. She did not know the handwriting either.

"Who could have sent it, *Mamá*?" she asked, turning the box to see if it had any other marks of identification. The man had said it came from the confectionery in Cidra, but he did not know who had bought it.

"Open it," said Grandmother, "and stop asking questions."

The box was filled with almonds, lollipops, rock candy and all sorts of cookies. There was an envelope addressed to her, and she recognized the handwriting.

"It's from *Papá!*" she cried, tearing open the envelope.

She read the note quickly. The expression that came upon her face was one of complete disappointment. She closed the box slowly.

"What is it, Teresa?" asked her mother.

"*Papá* won't be able to come to the closing of the feast. Business," she said.

"Whatever is detaining him must be important," said Grandmother, trying to cheer her granddaughter. "Rodrigo has never missed a closing or opening of the feast."

"What are you going to do with so much candy?" said her mother, trying to take her daughter's mind from the bad news. "You should see what Juana has for you, too."

But Teresa showed little interest. What could be keeping her father in town all day and part of the evening? Not to have him the very first time she was to conduct the feast, that was the worst possible thing that could happen to her. She laid the box on the kitchen table. Ramón was waiting for her to finish the carols. She felt all her previous enthusiasm leaving her. As she turned to go, Juana came into the kitchen, her arms full of packages. At the sight of Teresa, she stood still, not knowing what to do.

"Come along, Juana," said Doña Anita, "we have told Teresa already. Her father has disappointed her, and not even the sight of all the candy you have in those boxes will cheer her. What will ever happen to the feast tonight?"

Juana made room on the table for her packages and opened the boxes to let Teresa see their contents. There were all shapes and varieties in her selections of homemade candy, for which Juana was famous.

"Oh, Juana, they are just like the ones you made for Mercedes' birthday," said Teresa examining them. "Remember how surprised Mercedes was?"

"Will you help us make cornucopias to put them in, just like the ones we made for Mercedes? I would like one for every boy and girl who comes to the feast tonight."

Juana looked at the family and smiled. She got out a piece of blue ribbon from her pocket and gave it to Teresa. "It's from Sixta's sewing box. Her mother sent it to you to tie the cornucopias with. She wants Sixta to take part in the feast tonight, even if she's away."

"But where did you make all this candy, Juana?"

"At Sixta's home, so you would not find out."

"We will make the cornucopias for you," said her mother, glad to see Teresa's mood change for the best. "You and Ramón can fill them up with candy after you finish with the carols. There is not much time left."

When she joined Ramón, Antonio had already learned his part. She told them all about her father and the gift he had sent. She explained about Juana's candy and the cornucopias her mother was making for them. Then they went over their own carols until they, too, were sure of them.

There was still the lemonade to be made and the long table outside the kitchen door to be fixed. Everything else was done. The platters of cornbread, meat patties, crackers and cheese filled the wooden shelves of the kitchen.

When the sun went down, the family went to the shed. Ramón had added two extra chairs and placed a bouquet of flowers on each. Teresa took the small wreath from the leaves and added it to the bouquet on Ramón's chair.

They did not have to wait long before the workers began to arrive. They went throughout the shed, admiring the altar and commenting on the children's taste. There seemed to be the same air of festivity around as on the opening of the feast. The workers were curious as to whether the children could turn out a good ending for the feast. More and more workers came, accompanied by some of their friends, until the shed was filled. Again a group had to sit on the grass.

Teresa, Antonio and Ramón took their seats and waited for everyone to get settled. Teresa held the crystal beads in her hands, because she was going to conduct the rosary. The light of the single lantern fell on the Cross and made the rest of the altar look like a forest at twilight.

Teresa heard the children behind her say, "When are they going to start?" Trembling a little, she began to chant her opening. She pulled at Ramón's sleeves—for her voice seemed suddenly to be leaving her. She passed him the rosary, and his voice soon rose high and clear. When he had the group going through each decade and Teresa had regained her confidence, he passed her the beads again. She followed at ease now, on and on until she reached the end. Like Grandmother had done on the first night of the feast, Teresa led them in the singing of the *Adórate* and again the group burst into singing the many choruses they liked so well. When they finished and Teresa had reached the part where the carols came, Ramón nodded to Antonio. He took his small bouquet and walked to the altar, saying more than singing,

> Tulips and lilies I present
> And good wishes for all
> I beg of her.

He placed his bouquet on the altar and re-turned to his seat. He had done his part well.

Teresa followed. She sang loud and clear,

> Water for the valley
> And sun for our fields
> I ask from you, Oh Queen!
> That the earth may also partake of
>      your gifts,
> And the babbling brook
> That we love so well
> May join us in singing
> Your praises as well.

She laid down her flowers and sat down.

It was now Ramón's turn. Any other boy his size and age would have felt embarrassed to go through with it, but not Ramón. He walked boldly to the altar singing,

> Violets and hyacinths
> At your foot I lay
> Bringing to a close
> This floral feast of May.

Then he climbed up the ladder and slipped the tiny wreath over the Cross.

"*¡Viva la Cruz!*—Long live the Cross!" he shout-ed.

"*¡Viva! ¡Viva!*" the workers cried, overjoyed at what they had seen. The children's ending of the feast was an unusual one, they all had to agree.

Just then from somewhere came the sound of music, and a voice broke into a song. Teresa recognized the voice.

"It's *Papá!*" she cried, standing on her chair to place him among the crowd.

She saw him sitting under the trees, surrounded by Nicanor and two other musicians. Teresa ran out of the shed to join him.

"You did come back," she said. "You saw the end of the feast after all."

"I was busy all day looking for something special for tonight, and at last I found these three musicians."

"That was a fine closing you children had. I am proud of you."

There never was a celebration like the one at the *finca* that night. The workers ate and sang, and when the last of the food was gone, Don Rodrigo said the musicians would play for anyone who cared to dance. The bare ground soon filled with couples twirling and laughing, dancing under the stars and a moon that hung so low it looked unreal.

The children joined hands in a circle and ran about the place encircling people and making them pay a penalty by singing a song before they freed them. Once they even caught Grandmother. But their greatest fun came when Teresa brought out the cornucopias filled with candy and gave each of them one to take home.

When the workers began to get ready to leave, Teresa joined her parents at the head of the hill to say goodbye. She watched them go down, still humming some of the tunes they had heard the musicians play. She could hear the children's voices, too, as they called one another to hurry up. Once she heard the word *capia*. Were the children discussing next summer's feast? If they were, Teresa knew everyone was really hoping for a *capia*, and why shouldn't they? Maybe one of them would be selected, now that her mother had made it possible for children to join the feast.

On the way back, she stood by the shed for one more look at the altar. A ray of moonlight shone upon the steps, adding luster to the flowers buried in the moss. She thought of her promise to Filimón.

"I wish," she said softly, "that Filimón will always be the best driver of the land."

# CHAPTER 4
# POMAROSAS

Juana left the next day. Ramón and Teresa walked to the end of the country road with her and waited until the coach arrived. Don Rodrigo had reserved a seat for her early in the week, and since then she had been sure she would have to sit in the rear.

"There won't be another Filimón with whom to talk either," she told Teresa as she sat on a rock to wait.

Finally the coach arrived. Poor Juana, her fears were confirmed. Not only did she have to sit in the rear, but she had to force the woman who sat next to her to move the packages she had scattered on the seat. The woman seemed to resent her coming into the coach to disturb her comfort.

"Goodbye, Juana," said Ramón and Teresa as the coach departed. They stood waving until the coach was out of sight, then went back home to begin clearing out the shed.

Teresa wrapped up the mahogany cross and took it to the house while Ramón tore down the altar and the steps and took the wood to the wood-shed.

"Don't tear down the shed, Ramón. We can use it all summer long," said Teresa when she came back. "You can do your carving here and it will also make a good playhouse for Antonio and the children who always play with him."

They were interrupted by Don Rodrigo, who asked Ramón for his horse.

"Finish up, Teresa, I forgot your father has to go to the *finca* at once. Pile up the branches for me, and I'll throw them away when I return."

Teresa did not finish, but ran instead to her father and asked him to take her along with him to the *finca*.

"Two on a horse?" he asked, laughing.

"Yes, two on a horse," she answered.

"Two on a horse it shall be," he assured her.

This was the way Teresa had begun to ask for rides when she was a little girl. Her father could not resist trying the old routine.

When the horse was ready, Ramón helped Teresa to her place and returned to the shed.

There were several shortcuts to the *finca*, but Don Rodrigo took the one that he knew was Teresa's favorite, the one that led through a shallow stream to a narrow path shaded by trees. Teresa took a long breath. This was compensation enough after being away so long from home. This was a prelude to what the rest of her days at home would be. Now the *finca* was ahead, and she was riding once more with her father along her special road.

They reached the place where the old crooked tree stood. The horse brushed past it, and the heavy dew on its branches soaked their heads.

"That dew seemed more like a shower," said her father.

Teresa did not mind it. The horse crossed the stream and came out onto the main path.

"Ho! Don Rodrigo," called a group of boys from across the way.

"Ho!" he answered.

"Who are they?" asked Teresa.

"New tenants on the *finca*. Their fathers came to do some extra work this year and stayed over. Those children spend their time working for some of the farmers around here. When they are not working, they are walking back and forth from Cidra to Cayey."

When Don Rodrigo and Teresa came within view of the *finca*, Teresa asked her father to let her down so she could walk the rest of the way.

"Meet me at the overseer's home before noon," he said, leaving her standing in the center of the road.

How big the fields seemed after being away from them for a whole year. She stopped to watch the peasants in the fields. They all wore straw hats to protect them from the sun. Their loose shirt-waists fluttered in the wind as they worked among the furrows. She remembered the fruit farm she had seen on her way from the city, and the young boy who looked so much like Ramón. Here, too, some of the farm workers were gathering fruit with their baskets strapped to their backs.

Downhill was the overseer's house. If her friend Pilar was home, she would invite her to walk around the *finca*. She ran downhill towards the rear of the house.

The first thing one saw when approaching the house from that angle was the large cistern, where Pilar kept the rainwater for drinking purposes. She had planted *verbena* and *albahaca* plants around the base to hold the moisture and keep the water cool. Felipe had built a wood rack around it, where the ladders were hung.

"Pilar! Pilar!" she called, but no one answered.

She pushed the door open and looked in. The house was clean and neat. Pilar was a good house-keeper. There was a dishpan full of clean dishes on the table and a large basket full of starched clothes on the floor. Teresa guessed that Pilar was washing by the river. If she walked fast enough and met her before she started back home, they could walk to see the waterfall. Teresa closed the door and started downhill towards the river.

It was steep going down, and Teresa had to hold onto the branches of the bushes for balance. Once down the narrow path, she hurried along until she came to where a set of flat stones extended across the river. It was here where the peasants beat their clothes clean. The place was deserted. There were two empty baskets near some clothes drying in the sun. Could it have been Pilar? And if so, where could she have gone? If it had been Pilar, she was probably in the natural pool bathing. Teresa had been with her there before.

Teresa left the river path and turned towards the cluster of bushes that closed the entrance to the pool. She heard the waterfall long before she parted the bushes. The place was as deserted as the river. She stood watching the water drop into the hollow stone that formed the pool and go over its brim. She followed its course under the thicket on its way to the many rivulets throughout the land. She was sure that somewhere the waterfall met the river, although she did not know where.

"I have missed Pilar," she said to herself, "but I will not miss a dip in this pool." The water was colder than she expected and she swam below the surface to increase her circulation. A puff of wind sent a number of fruit plopping into the water. They were small, pink *pomarosas* fruit. She tried to fill her hands with them, but the light fruit bobbed and floated always ahead of her and out of reach. Another gust of wind brought down a larger number. She jumped from the water and dressed quickly.

The *pomarosas* were all over the ground as well as on the surface of the water. She took a handful and sat on the grass to eat them, throwing the brown pits over the pool. The force of the waterfall made the fruit float faster and faster, and soon the *pomarosas* went bobbing over the brim and out under the thicket where rivulets ran. They seemed like small apricots to her, except that they were hollow inside with a small brown pit rolling around inside.

"I wish I had a basket to take some of them home," she said, beginning to gather as many *pomarosas* as she could carry in both hands.

Teresa left the pool as the sound of her father's voice reached her. It was coming from far away, yet she heard it distinctively.

"Teresaaaaa! Teresaaaaa!" over and over he called. She began to run towards the river path, wondering if it could be noon time. She remembered she had promised to meet him at Pilar's home.

"Teresaaaaa, Teresaaaaa, Teresaaaaa!" she heard again, only this time there seemed to be more than one person calling her. She ran faster and faster, holding the *pomarosas* close in her hands. Suddenly, the bushes across the river began to shake furiously, and she heard the sound of crushing dead branches underfoot. A stray goat or a dog, she thought. What if it was Leal, Ramón's dog? She stopped. Whatever it was had to come out into the open, for that was the end of the row of bushes. When the branches parted, she did not see Leal, nor a goat, but the face of a strange man. She dropped the *pomarosas* and ran up the path. When she reached the part where the flat stones were, she saw Felipe running towards her.

"Where were you?" he asked. "Your father and I have been looking for you everywhere. One of the prisoners working on the road has escaped, and they say he's headed for this *finca*."

"I have been looking for Pilar," said Teresa.

She went to town early this morning," said Felipe. "That's why we've been worrying about you."

As he finished talking, four civil guards came running towards them.

"Where did he go? Have you seen him?" they asked.

"I don't know," answered Felipe. "I haven't seen anyone."

"But I did," said Teresa. "There is someone hiding in those bushes across the river."

The guards leaped into the water, skipping over the flat stones until they reached the opposite side. They disappeared behind the shrubbery and had not been gone very long when a sharp whistle blew and shouts of "Aquí, aquí" were heard.

Felipe and Teresa knew the guards had completed their mission.

"Let's go home, Teresa," said Felipe, and the two hurried along, eager to reach the house before the guard reappeared.

When they arrived, they saw Don Rodrigo riding downhill.

"Where did you find her?" he asked, jumping off his horse.

"Running by the river path," said Felipe. "She had just seen the prisoner across the river."

"Seen the fugitive?" he asked, mopping his brow nervously.

It was then that he noticed her wet braids and knew she had been bathing in the pool.

Don Rodrigo seldom forbade Teresa anything, but this he now knew. She should never bathe alone in that pool again. She nodded when he told her.

"Of all the *fincas* about the place, why did he have to choose ours?" she said.

"Choose is the wrong word to use," said her father. "It was his safety he was thinking of, just as much as I am thinking of yours. Now let us go home."

They rode back without a word between them, although both were thinking about the same thing.

As they entered the family path, the sound of the conch shell reached them.

"Lunch," said her father. "I can eat for two after all the riding I have done."

But Teresa knew that the best cooking at home could not lure her to eat.

# CHAPTER 5
# MERCEDES

Antonio had come to the house earlier than usual to ask Teresa about her adventure the day before. So far, he had not been able to see her. Teresa was in the neck, helping the family sew the edges of a tablecloth, a present for her aunt in San Juan which she would take her when school time came again. Antonio had received the mail before coming to the door. With two letters and a catalog, he walked triumphantly, purposefully into the neck, confident of his pretext.

"The mail," he said, handing Doña Anita the two letters and putting the catalog on Don Rodrigo's table.

One of the letters was addressed to Doña Anita, and she turned it over quickly to see whom it was from. There was no return address.

"Is it from Aunt Elvira?" Teresa asked, noticing the postmark from San Juan on the envelope.

"I wish it was," said her mother, "but this is not her handwriting."

She opened the envelope, pulled out the letter and glanced at the signature before she began to read its contents.

"Why, it is from Lucio." She read on and then stopped. "I better read this aloud. The news concerns us all. Listen:

Dear friend:

The following goes to you hoping it will find the family well, and to ask a favor. Will it be possible for Mercedes to stay at the *finca*, while I go around the island on important business?

In the event that I don't hear from you to the contrary, we will be there Saturday of this week.

Your friend,
Lucio

"Mercedes is coming here at last," Teresa said enthusiastically.

"Say it will be all right, *Mamá*. She can share my room."

"Of course," her mother assented, "but I don't think she will have to share your room. We can have the small one adjoining yours ready for her."

"Answer the letter first," suggested Grandmother. "There is time to decide about the room later on. Bring paper and ink, Teresa."

After the letter was written and dispatched to Lucio, Teresa and her mother went to inspect the small room. Antonio, who had not forgotten his purpose, followed them.

The room was the smallest in the house, but the view from its only window was rewarding. The room was empty, except for a single bed standing in the center.

"Oh, dear," said Doña Anita, "we will have to improvise a closet for her. This room looks as bare as a cell."

"I saw a small cabinet with four drawers in the woodshed when Ramón and I were putting away the steps from the altar. Why couldn't we use it? Perhaps I can find other things suitable for the room."

"Go and see, but remember the size of the room. Do not bring up any useless things. Mercedes must have some room to move around."

"Come along with me, Antonio," said Teresa.

"At last I will be able to ask her," he thought as he followed her to the woodshed. Before she opened the door, he had asked his question about her adventure with the escaped convict.

Teresa broke into a loud laugh. "Where did you hear such a story, Antonio?"

"But did you really capture him?" he asked, disregarding her question.

"No, no, Antonio," she answered impatiently.

"That's what Manolo said, but I said you did," Antonio insisted.

Teresa laughed again. She could well picture Antonio standing up for her in front of his friend Manolo, only this time Antonio was wrong.

"Do you really want to know the truth?" she asked him. "I only saw the fugitive from across the river, and when I did, I ran from there as fast as I could."

"Were you afraid?" he asked.

"I certainly was."

She pushed the door of the shed open and went in. Antonio shrugged his shoulders and turned to a pile of papers in a corner. He found a discarded seed catalog and began to flip the pages. "Whoever heard of being afraid of a man across the river?" he said to himself, dismissing the entire affair from his mind.

Teresa found the cabinet and began to empty the drawers. Now and then she glanced at Antonio, glad she had put an end to his questioning. She too had tried to forget the scare she had received, promising herself not to discuss it ever again. She was certain Antonio would not be able to enlarge on her version of the incident, for there was no doubt he was disappointed. He would not even mention it to Manolo. Antonio was a poor loser.

In addition to the cabinet, there were two small stools and an oval grass rug which could be used in the room. She found a discarded table which she would have liked to have, but was sure her mother would not approve.

"Carry this rug for me, Antonio," she said. "There's nothing else here I want."

When they came back to the room, Lucía had swept and scrubbed the floor and pushed the small bed near the wall. Grandmother had left one of her colorful spreads for it.

"Where shall I put the rug?" asked Antonio, holding the catalog he had brought with him.

"In front of the bed," said Teresa. "Now you can tell Mercedes that you helped fix her room."

"Who is Mercedes?"

"My best friend."

"I thought Sixta was that."

"Of course she is, but so is Mercedes."

Antonio looked puzzled.

"Look," said Teresa, trying to make it clear. "It's like having Esteban and Ramón for friends. Aren't they both your best friends?"

Antonio assented quickly.

"Well, so are Sixta and Mercedes, except that one lives in the city and the other on the *finca*."

Apparently satisfied, Antonio went back to his catalog and left Teresa to her work.

At dinner time Doña Anita asked Ramón not to go to work the next day in order to help finish the work needed in the room. She wanted him to make a closet like the one he had improvised for his room.

There was the cabinet in the woodshed, which Teresa had selected and wanted painted. He and Teresa could do that while Doña Anita sewed a cretonne curtain for the closet.

So the work which had begun as soon as Lucio's letter had arrived continued all week until the small room was ready. The cabinet was painted yellow and placed under the window. A closet was improvised with blue wooden pegs for hangers and a creton curtain that rolled back and forth and would keep the dust off Mercedes' clothes. It had been hard work, but working together, as they had done, had also been a great deal of fun.

The day before Mercedes' arrival was a rainy day, and when the family awoke the next morning it was still raining.

"What a day to come to the *finca*," said Teresa, drawing a chair close to the window. Everytime the wheels of a coach rattled on the road, she would jump to see if the coach was turning onto their private path. But the morning passed and part of the afternoon as well, and still Mercedes did not come.

"It's no use," her grandmother said. "Who would be traveling on a day like this?"

Mercedes would, thought Teresa, and so would I if I were coming to a *finca*.

"One day is as good as another," her mother said. "They will probably come tomorrow."

All their remarks could not discourage Teresa, who remained at her post even after her father and Ramón had left to write up the catalog orders for things needed at the *finca*. Her mother and grandmother had gone back to the kitchen. Teresa looked out the windows. The branches of the trees hung heavy with the dripping rain. She thought of the many times when as a small child she had sung, "Rain, rain, go away, come again some other day," and had waited for the miracle to happen, confident that it would be as she had hoped.

Was that the sound of wheels she heard? She listened closely. It was a coach. She could see it between the branches of the trees. It turned off the road and entered the path leading to the gate. The curtains were drawn and fastened, and Teresa could not see the occupants, but she was sure who they were, for the coach had stopped and Filimón had jumped off his seat to open the door.

"*Papá, Mamá!*" she cried, "they have come; they are at the gate this very minute.

Armed with umbrellas, Don Rodrigo and Ramón made their way down the slippery hill to the gate, where Filimón was busy unfastening the oil-cloth curtains.

Teresa hung out of the window, waving and calling to Mercedes, who had poked her head out of the coach.

"Wait for the umbrellas," she cried. "Don't leave the coach."

When Ramón and Don Rodrigo arrived, Mercedes quickly got under Ramón's umbrella.

"You must be Ramón," she said. "I would have known you anywhere, so good has Teresa described you."

"You better hold on tight to my arm. This hill is very slippery," Ramón said.

Lucio and Don Rodrigo followed. "We had given you up completely," said Don Rodrigo, "except, of course, Teresa. I don't think she doubted for a minute that you would get here. She has watched the road all morning and afternoon."

"Welcome! Welcome!" said the family when they reached the house.

Grandmother took one look at their shoes, heavy with mud, and brought wet newspapers to wipe them off.

Teresa was discouraged to hear Mercedes had not seen the road children nor visited the country store. When Filimón brought the trunk, she took Mercedes along to show her the room. They passed the dining room and entered the neck.

"There is the conch shell," cried Mercedes. "Are we on the other part of the house already?"

"Yes," said Teresa. "There is Grandmother's room over there. Mine is the one across, and this one is to be yours."

She stepped aside to let Filimón set the trunk down.

"How do you like it?" she asked when Filimón had gone.

"It's the smallest room I have ever seen. It looks like a room in a large doll's house."

Mercedes examined the closet with the blue pegs and the cabinet under the window.

"I like this closet," she said. "All I have to do is roll off the curtain instead of having to open and close doors. Oh, Teresa, I do like the room, and you have done so much to make it look pretty."

Teresa was pleased. "I hope you will like the *finca* just as well. Then you will come every summer to stay with us. This will always be your room."

"Do you want to unpack your trunk now?" she asked. "I can help you put the things away?"

Mercedes took out the key to her trunk, opened the trunk and began to sort the things that were to go into the drawers and those she wanted hung in the closet.

"May I help, too?" someone said at the door.

"Why, Sixta, when did you come home?" Teresa pulled her friend in and introduced her to Mercedes.

"I came home last night. *Mamá* told me about Mercedes' visit. So today when I saw the coach pass by, I decided to come and see her. I'm glad you came to the *finca*, Mercedes. Teresa has spoken of you all summer long."

Mercedes had not expected to find Sixta such a grown-up person. She thought she looked older than her nineteen years. Perhaps it was because, as Teresa had said, she had worked so hard in order to be able to go to school.

Sixta was laughing now, telling Teresa about some of her experiences at school, and Mercedes noticed how her face had changed. Why, she was no more the serious girl she had seemed a minute earlier. She had turned into an excited schoolgirl, with a radiant face and a warm look in her eyes. Mercedes liked her open frankness. It would be easy to be friends with a girl like her, despite her being older. No wonder Teresa liked her so much.

"Would you like to hang up my dresses, Sixta?" she asked her. "Teresa and I can start to put these things away in the cabinet."

They talked back and forth as they worked, telling Mercedes little tales about the *finca* and assuring her that the sun did shine most of the time, regardless of the two days of rain they had had.

Leal's barking and Antonio's shouts brought Teresa to the door. Antonio was running through the neck, followed by Leal barking at his heels and Filo walking slowly at a respectable distance.

"Don't bring them here, Antonio," cried Teresa.

But the three had come to stay. Leal nosed Mercedes while Filo purred and meowed softly on the other side of the bed. Mercedes and Sixta took turns sharing Leal's affection as he jumped and frolicked about the room. Filo's meowing grew louder and louder.

"They are jealous of each other," explained Teresa. "If you pet one, you must pet the other."

"Here, here, Filo," said the girls, rubbing Filo's gray fur. The cat arched her back and stiffened her tail until it looked like a mast.

Mercedes sat on one of the stools and took her onto her lap, where she settled contentedly.

"Now you have met everyone in the family," said Doña Anita, coming into the room, "even Antonio, but I advise you to keep these two pets out of here if you want to save your grass mat. There won't be a piece of it left. Now follow me. Lucía has dinner ready."

Sixta tried to get out of it by suggesting they remain to finish putting Mercedes' things away, but neither Teresa nor her mother would hear of it. So Sixta followed them to the dining room.

As soon as they sat down to dinner, Lucio began to talk about his trip. "If I can get enough land," he said, "and enough tobacco planters interested in my plan, you will see the first association of tobacco planters and manufacturers on the island. You ought to consider it seriously, Rodrigo. It's men like you that I am after."

"It sounds interesting," he said. "I would like to give it some thought."

The family was carried away with Lucio's project, and Sixta thought it would benefit the island as a whole.

Teresa thought she had heard enough, so she motioned to Mercedes to follow her. They returned to their work. Teresa knew that Lucio's topic of conversation would be the subject for hours and hours.

Once back at the room, they set to work once more. Mercedes took out a box from the bottom of the trunk.

"Here's cousin Flora's gift. Where shall I put it, Teresa?"

"What is it?" asked Teresa.

Mercedes took the lid off to show the contents of the box. Inside was a pin and needle cushion, plus a series of cardboard sections with pins, spools of threads, buttons, safety pins, rolls of narrow ribbon and two tiny sachets.

"Where did cousin Flora think you were going, to a desert?" said Teresa, impressed with the fitted box.

Mercedes laughed. "You don't know my cousin. She has even given me a pair of white shoes. Imagine! White shoes for a *finca*!"

"Better put this box on top of the cabinet. I hate to think of the work we'll have to do if we drop it and upset its contents."

"What did my teacher say when you brought her my letter, Mercedes?"

"Oh," she said, "you must have known about the Feast of the Cross all the time. That was why you had worked as you did to make the list of exemptions and get home on time."

"She said that? Well, that was as good a reason as any, but that really was not true. It just happened that Grandmother's letter arrived at the same time the list went up."

"I wish you had been here for the feast. I made the *capias* this summer. Every night the altar was prettier and prettier, and on the last night, do you know what happened?"

"What?" Mercedes asked, putting her comb and brush on the cabinet and then settling on a stool.

"Mother gave three *capias*: one to Ramón, one to Antonio and one to me!"

"*Capias* for children? I never heard of that before," said Mercedes.

"Neither did the workers, nor we, for that matter. Anyhow, we did have fun fixing the altar and composing the carols. The surprise of the evening was Father. He brought three musicians and suggested that the peasants dance."

"And did they?"

"Of course, and sang all kinds of songs, besides."

"How I wish you could come and see the feast sometime. Perhaps next year. You're going into the seventh grade and can try for the exemption list. I have to try for the eighth grade one, too, if I want to get here in time again. Next time my teacher will be right."

"*Ay,*" said Mercedes, "that will mean working twice as hard for one."

They had not realized that the sound of the rain on the roof had stopped and that the room had become dim, so absorbed had they been in their talk. When they rejoined the family, the gas lamps were already lit. Ramón, Don Rodrigo and Lucio were busy with a catalog while Sixta, Doña Anita and Grandmother were examining a new crochet pattern. The night had turned cool after the rain, and Grandmother had wrapped her warm shawl around her shoulders. A ray of light shot through the darkness outside, and thousands of lights began to dance outside the door.

"Fireflies! Fireflies!" cried Mercedes. "I have never seen so many all at once. Let's count them."

"You can't count fireflies," said Teresa. "Look, there seems to be twice as many already. Father calls them the magic light of the *finca.*"

Don Rodrigo pushed his chair back and closed the catalog. "Come, Grandmother," he said, "how about a story? The fireflies have come to welcome Mercedes, and we can't do much less."

"Yes, yes, Grandmother," they all begged. "A story, a story."

Grandmother thought for a while, trying to find a tale suitable for all.

"Do you like mangoes, Mercedes?" she asked.

"I do, especially if they are from Mayagüez," she answered.

"Then a story about mangoes it shall be. Listen."

"It was the eve of the Feast of the good St. John. And in a small house in the interior of the island three sisters sat pondering what to do on such a night—a night endowed with all kinds of magic possibilities."

"'I am going to cut out an alphabet,' said Tita, who was the eldest, 'and fold each letter firmly before dropping it into a basin of water. At midnight, I'll find open the letters which spell out the name of my future husband.'

"'I will prepare the three garlics,' said Nona, the second sister. 'One whole head for a rich husband, one half for a merchant's son and one fourth for a beggar. At midnight, I shall draw out one and we shall see what we shall see.'

'I will break an egg in a glass of water,' said Clarita, the youngest sister. 'At midnight it will have turned into my future.'

"So each sister set to her task, and though they retired early to bed, not a wink did they sleep all night. When the clock struck twelve, up they rose and ran to see what the future held for them.

"Of Tita's alphabet, four letters had opened. She put them quickly together. They spelled out *'Bobo.'* Now, she knew that a *bobo* was nothing but a simpleton. Thinking that her future foretold her marriage to a simpleton, she began to cry.

"'I won't marry a simpleton. I won't, I won't,' she said and went back to bed to cry herself to sleep.

"Nona searched for her garlics in the small box where she had carefully set them aside. Closing her eyes she drew one out.

"'A half garlic,' she proclaimed joyously. `That suits me well.'

"Clarita brought out her glass to the light. Lo and behold! The yolk of the egg had turned burnt orange in color and had adhered to one side of the glass while the white part had taken the shape of a miniature boat with tiny masts as fine as threads.

"'I am going away from home,' she said softly. 'This boat is sailing away at the setting of the sun.' She replaced the glass carefully on the table and sat looking at the tiny boat.

"'Where shall you take me, little boat, and who shall the captain be?' she asked almost in a whisper. Finally, she went back to bed and soon fell asleep.

"Time passed, but the sisters did not forget the fortunes foretold that night. One day they heard that on a faraway hill on the other side of the mountain was a grove where a strange fruit grew. Eager to see for themselves, they started one morning in search of it. On and on they walked past valleys and mountains, and though the rays of the hot sun beat upon them and their feet grew tired, they did not stop until they had come to the most beautiful hill they had ever seen. There were rare flowers everywhere, and in the center of the hill was a circle of trees whose branches were laden heavy with a large fruit. Some of them were still green, others rich golden yellow, while others were partly green and partly red as a rose. Some of the ripe fruit had dropped from the tree and had scattered on the grass.

"'If we could only have trees like these on our hill,' said the sisters. They picked some of the fruit off the grass and began to eat it. They had never tasted fruit like that before, nor was its taste similar to any other fruit they knew. Even the seed they found inside was rare: large, with fibers long and fine as hair.

"'Let us carry some of this fruit home,' said Clarita. 'We can plant these seeds on our hill and care for them so that they might take root.'

"She took off her apron and began to fill it with fruit. Suddenly, they heard voices. Coming towards them were three young men.

"'Oh!' cried Clarita, dropping the apron and spilling the fruit about her feet.

"'Who are you?' asked the young men, surprised to see strangers in their grove.

"'We are sisters,' said Tita, 'we live by the side of the mountain. News of the rare fruit that grows here reached us, and we came to see for ourselves.'

"'Hour after hour we have walked to reach this hill,' said Nona. 'Our trip was well rewarded. This is the most beautiful hill we have ever seen. But who are you?'

"'We, too, are brothers,' said the young men, 'and we live on this hill. These are mangoes, the most precious fruit that grows in our land.'

"They noticed the apron on the ground and the fruit scattered about it. 'If it's fruit you want,' said one of the brothers, 'pick all you can carry. The crop is abundant and often goes to waste.' Then without another word, the three brothers continued on their way.

"Each of the sisters took off their aprons, filled them with fruit and they, too, went away.

"As time went on, the three brothers spoke of nothing else but the three sisters from across the mountain. The three sisters in turn paused often in their housework to discuss the three brothers from up the hill.

"One fine morning, the three brothers decided upon a plan. They would go out in search of the three sisters and ask their hands in marriage. It was a long walk through unknown roads. They climbed down hills and walked through paths lined with great trees. They crossed field after field and finally came to a mountain.

"'This must be the mountain the sisters mentioned,' said one of the brothers.

"'Their house must be not far,' said another. 'Let us not stop, but walk ahead.'

"Down the mountain path they came to a small house surrounded by trees and a large backyard. Pits similar to the ones from the mangoes that grew in their grove were scattered everywhere.

"'This must be the house. Those are pits from our mangoes.'

"'Let's knock,' said one of the brothers.

"Great was their surprise when Tita, the eldest sister, came out.

"'I am Bobo,' said the eldest of the brothers. 'It is I who owns the hill where the rare fruit grows. If you accept me, the hill and the fruit will be your own.'

"Nona heard voices and came to see who had come to call on them.

"'I am Perico,' said the second brother. 'It is I who upon marriage will inherit my father's business. If you accept me, you will become a rich merchant's wife.'

"Now, Clarita, the youngest sister, had been busy cooking in the kitchen and had not heard the brothers knock. Needing some bay leaves for seasoning, she opened the door to ask one of her sisters to pick them from the garden when she noticed the three brothers. Off came the pot from the charcoal fire and she too joined her sisters in the outer room.

"'I am Ramiro,' said the youngest brother. 'It is I who owns the frigate now on the bay. Twice a year I come back to the hill. If you accept me, you too will sail away, and twice a year will come back home with me.'

"The sisters looked at each other and remembered the fortunes told that night long ago on the eve of the good St. John.

"'What shall we do?' whispered Clarita to her sister Nona.

"Before Nona had time to answer, Tita, who had heard the question and was now glad she did not have to marry a simpleton after all, whispered back, 'Let us accept them, of course.'

"So they did, and the three sisters married the three brothers.

"Tita went to live up on the hill and became the owner of the hill and its rare fruits. Nona stayed in the house at the bottom of the hill, and together with Perico planted the pits scattered about the yard.

"In time tiny shrubs began to grow all about the yard, and it was not long before she too had mangoes like the ones Tita had in her grove on the hill.

"But Clarita sailed away with Ramiro to strange lands. Twice a year she returned home, and then, under the shade of the mango trees, she told her sisters about her travels, the strange scenes and the foreign people she had seen."

"That was a fine story, Grandmother," said Don Rodrigo.

"*Mamá* thinks the hill the sisters found with the mango trees is right here, on the *finca*," said Doña Anita.

"Do you really think so?" asked Mercedes.

"No, I don't really know," Grandmother said, "but I always have wanted it to be. There is a mango grove not far from here, you know."

"There is? Oh, Teresa, when can we go to see it?"

"When you do," said Sixta, "tell us if you find anything besides mangoes there." Saying this, she picked up her umbrella from the large earthenware jug at the corner of the room and said good night to the family.

"Who would like to walk down with Sixta?" asked Doña Anita.

"We will," said Teresa. "Then Mercedes can really see how the *finca* looks at night. Come along, Ramón."

# CHAPTER 6
# PIG STY

Next morning, Mercedes awoke with a start.

Outside, the air was full of music. She flung the shutters of her window wide open. Perched on a branch of a tree which grazed the wall was a myriad of small birds, the likes of which she had not seen before. It was as if they were saluting the new day with their songs.

Mercedes stood wide-eyed, watching their tiny beaks and the throbbing of their chests as they sang. This no doubt was their favorite branch, for no sooner were they gone than a new group flew down, chirping and twittering and bursting into song.

"This is awakening on a *finca*," thought Mercedes, used to the common song of the morning vendor in the city and the clatter of his wheelbarrow on the cobbled street.

A gleam of yellow light touched the mountain in the far distance and soon spread over hill and valley, outlining the houses scattered far below.

A woman and a boy were making their way slowly up the hill. For them, too, the day had begun.

Two knocks sounded on the partition separating her room from Teresa's. She quickly answered back. Before she had finished dressing, Teresa was in her room.

"*Buenos días*, Mercedes," she said cheerfully. "The sun is out. Now we can go walking about the place."

Teresa looked out the window. The woman and the boy had reached the top of the hill and were approaching the shed.

"Why, there is Lucía and Antonio. It must be later than I thought. Come along, let's get our breakfast before the rest of the family gets up."

They tiptoed out of the room and went through the neck past the dining room and into the kitchen.

"*Buenos días*," said Lucía, surprised to see them up so early. "Teresa is making sure you get the best air of the *finca*, Mercedes. That's what I always tell my Antonio: the fresh morning air is the best air of the *finca*."

"Give us something to eat, Lucía," said Teresa. "We are going out walking."

"May I come along?" said Antonio.

Lucía busied herself around the kitchen, trying to get something for the children that would not take too much time. When she had it ready, the children sat around the kitchen table more interested in discussing places to see than in eating the crackers, bananas and cheese, and drinking the cocoa she had served them.

Antonio wanted to go one way and Teresa wanted to go another. At last, they compromised. Teresa would lead the way and Antonio would bring them back whichever way he wanted. In that case, Mercedes would not be seeing the same things twice.

Teresa walked downhill to the main road and went past the large old trees whose tangled roots on the surface of the ground were large enough to sit on.

"These are the oldest trees in the *finca*," said Teresa, pulling down one of the many vines that crept up the trunk.

When they were passing a barbed-wire fence covered with wild strawberries, Mercedes stopped to pick some of the fruit.

"They are sour," said Antonio. "No one eats them but the birds."

"These are not all sour. This one is sweet, and so is this one," said Mercedes, eating one after the other. But the rest she picked were not only sour but bitter, and she had to throw them away. Antonio knew what he was talking about.

"There's Sixta's home," said Teresa.

"Ho, Esteban!" called Antonio, running to the field.

"Looking for Sixta?" asked Esteban.

The door to the house opened and Sixta and her mother came out to greet them.

"I heard Antonio call Esteban, but I did not know he had company," said Sixta. "Mother tells me he does his rounds daily."

"I am going to be a farmer like Esteban and Ramón," said Antonio.

"Those were fine potatoes you dug," said Esteban. "Next time you come, you must pick the beans and the peppers and tomatoes."

"I cut potato eyes for Felipe last week," Antonio interrupted. "He says I can cut them faster than Manolo."

"He can read fast now, too," said Teresa. "Grandmother has helped him."

"Why don't you come along, Sixta?" asked Mercedes.

Sixta shook her head. She had work to do making lace on order for stores, and needed every minute of her time. Later on during the summer, perhaps they could even have a picnic together, but now she had to organize her work for the patrons in Cayey.

They said goodbye and continued their way, running ahead to the tamarind tree down the road. The ground was covered with pods, and they soon began to select the best ones they could find.

Antonio stuffed his pockets full.

"This is the only sweet tamarind tree in the *finca*," said Teresa.

"Taste one of the pods and you'll see," said Antonio.

Mercedes remembered the strawberries and hoped Antonio was right. They actually were sweet, and she hurried to gather more.

They left the main road and walked over dry leaves and branches towards a little clearing beyond. A large number of butterflies took off from the ferns that bordered the place.

"I want some," cried Mercedes, running after them. But no matter how high she jumped to catch them, the butterflies were always ahead of her.

"Get her one, Antonio," said Teresa.

"How can you catch them so easy?" said Mercedes when he brought her a large specimen that he called a rainbow butterfly. He spread its wings so that she could see the colors.

"Let it go," said Teresa. "We must go on."

He opened his hand and the butterfly fluttered away, soon lost among the ferns.

"Ramón taught me how to get them," said Antonio. "Maybe he can teach you, too."

"Have you tried, Teresa?" asked Mercedes.

"Of course, but I can't get them as easy as Ramón or Antonio."

Beyond the clearing was a small banana grove. It was apparently a bird's paradise, for the bananas on the ground and many on the trees showed the imprint of bird beaks. There were a variety of bananas, including long and thin ones that ripen quickly. There were also *guineos niños*, the finger-length ones that taste so good with cheese or fried eggs. And the fat, red ones the peasants say are for medicinal purposes only. Antonio enjoyed them until he ate so many that he was sick for months. Since then he never touched them again.

Teresa lead Mercedes through the grove, jumping over fallen branches and over fallen bananas clear across to the other side.

"Close your eyes," she said, "and don't open them until I say so."

It was from here that you got the best view of the *finca*.

"Now," said Teresa.

"The *finca* seems to stretch away to the very sky," said Mercedes when she opened her eyes.

Teresa pointed to the tobacco plots in the far distance, and the brown spots about the place, which were the tobacco sheds. She also pointed to the peasant houses across the hill, and even beyond to the shrubs that concealed the spring.

"I hope someone will take us riding through there someday," said Teresa. "Then you can see the river and the flat stones where the peasants do their laundry."

They sat under a tree to rest. The sun was rising and with it the heat of the day.

"I can see now why you want to come back to the *finca* as soon as school closes," said Mercedes. "If I had a *finca* like this, I would also want to be here all the time."

"Don't you like the city?" asked Antonio.

"Of course," said Mercedes, "but a city is not like a *finca*."

"I wish I could see San Juan," said Antonio, "with its fortresses and the sea all around it. Teresa tells me things about it sometimes."

When they stood up to go, Antonio led the way back home. He cut through the banana grove and ran up a narrow path, which they discovered was wired on both sides. It looked like an abandoned trail.

"If you are going to run all the way, better get on the road," called Teresa, running after him. They caught up with him at the end of the path. There were three rows of barbed wire running across it, and they had to part the wire carefully in order to go under it. Teresa's dress caught on it and tore.

"See here, Antonio," she cried, "are you sure you know the way?"

Antonio did not answer. He was on the run again.

"Antonio!" called Mercedes, "we can't follow you unless we see which way you are going."

They saw him circle some of the bushes, whistling merrily as if he were leading a game of hide and seek.

"Hurry! Hurry!" he called back at them.

"He thinks we are rabbits," said Teresa, "and expects us to squeeze under wire fences and scamper after him."

"I am not going to follow him anymore."

"There must be some other way out of this path," said Mercedes.

"Of course, there is," said Antonio, suddenly appearing along the side of the path.

He parted some of the branches and pointed to a house on a hill.

"Why, it's home," Teresa explained. "How did you ever find such a shortcut, wire fences and all?"

But Antonio was gone again. This time to meet Ramón, who was coming with two pails in his hands.

Teresa and Mercedes followed him.

"I am on my way to feed the pigs. It's fun to watch." He looked at Mercedes and smiled. "Would you like to come?"

"Ugh," said Teresa pulling at her nose. "Who wants to go to the pig sty?"

"I do," said Antonio, taking one of the pails from Ramón.

"Me, too," said Mercedes.

Teresa watched them go and then reluctantly followed them also.

As they approached the sty, they could hear the grunting of the pigs.

"They must know it's time to eat," said Mercedes.

"They do," said Antonio. "Pigs can always tell."

As soon as they went in, the pigs scurried towards the pen where they knew Ramón always left their noonday meal. At the head of the line came the fat sow. Every time one of the small pigs tried to get ahead, she would stop and block the way.

"You hungry wolf," said Ramón. "Haven't you sense to let the small ones come first? Someday, I am going to let you fast. It will be good penance for your greediness. Move...away with you."

The big sow reared and let out a squeal that frightened Mercedes.

"Look out, Ramón," she called, running to the gate.

"Don't be afraid," said Teresa. "She can't harm you."

"She might bite," Mercedes insisted, keeping her distance.

"Nonsense," said Ramón. "Watch me."

He shoved the sow out of the way without a problem. The rest of the pigs lined up alongside the pen and began to eat.

There was rhythm in the even movement of their heads, the twitching of their stumpy tails and the constant shifting of their hind legs. Only the sow stood still, watching Ramón's movements with her slanted eyes.

"Please give her something to eat, Ramón," said Antonio. "She needs to eat, too."

"I saved her share. She'll eat after the small pigs do," Ramón said emphatically.

"Let her eat with the rest," said Teresa. "Empty her food in this corner of the pen."

They emptied the pail while Ramón walked to where the sow stood. "Come on," he said, patting her back.

The sow grunted and squealed louder than ever, but would not move. He tried to pull her, but she stood her ground.

"Make a noose with that rope in the corner," said Antonio. "That's what Manolo's father does when his sow won't move."

Ramón fashioned a noose and threw it over her head, but the noose was too big and the sow wriggled her head out. Once free, she trotted around the pen, followed by Ramón and Antonio. In one of the turns, Ramón seized a hind leg and tried to hold her, but the sow shook herself free, sending Ramón rolling in the mud. Antonio tripped and fell over him. From the corner where they stood, Teresa and

Mercedes shook with laughter, and the small pigs squealed louder and louder.

Ramón and Antonio picked themselves up from the dirt floor.

"Try the noose again," said Antonio.

"It didn't do much good before," said Teresa.

"Look out," shouted Mercedes, "here she comes."

But the sow was apparently satisfied and walked calmly to the end of the pen. From there she turned to them with almost a triumphant look. Slowly she bent her head and tasted the sweet potatoes the girls had dumped. Her snout wriggled with the excitement of that first taste.

The rest of the pigs that had stopped eating before now reassumed. Soon all tails were again twitching and hind legs were stamping in unison.

"Pick up the pails, Antonio," said Ramón.

At the sound of his voice, the sow stopped eating and let out another of her squeals.

"*Cielos*," said Teresa, "let's leave the queen to her castle before she runs us all out."

When they came out into the open air, the intensity of the heat had reached its height. They walked slowly uphill and went back to the kitchen, where Lucía had lunch ready for them.

# CHAPTER 7
# WORK CAN BE FUN

As time went on and Mercedes became a part of the household, Teresa's responsibilities about the house lessened, so that the two girls had more time to roam about the *finca*.

Early mornings, they fed chickens, sorted beans and shelled peas. They saw that the ears of dry corn were strung on the rafters in the stockroom. On Saturday mornings they helped tend to the workers who came to do their shopping at the *finca* stockroom, which was a kind of store for them.

The stockroom opened early. Teresa managed the window, taking their orders and entering their account on a ledger book. It was her duty to keep these accounts up to date, for it was from them that her father calculated the workers' weekly salaries.

Ramón and Mercedes wrapped up the groceries, and Antonio took them to the peasants who stood outside the window.

One Saturday morning, after a trip to Cidra, Mercedes overslept. Although Teresa tapped at her wall on the way down to the stockroom, she did not wake. When she finally showed up, they were almost through with the line of peasants who had come to get their weekly groceries. Mercedes went to the table to help Ramón finish up the last orders.

"You and Antonio deserted us," said Ramón. "You should have seen us a few minutes ago. We even put Manolo to work. He was just as good as Antonio delivering the packages."

Mercedes shot a glance at Teresa, who was entering the account of the last worker in the ledger book. This was the first time she had missed helping her, and she promised herself that it would be the last. She brought the last package she had wrapped and gave it to the waiting worker herself.

"I am sorry, Teresa," she said.

Teresa closed the ledger book and shut the window.

"Let us know in advance when you intend to sleep all morning," she said, laughing. "I didn't know the air in Cidra would make a door mouse out of you. Grandmother wants to see us. Come along."

Grandmother was in the shed getting ready to start making bobbin-pin lace.

"You are just in time to help wind the thread around the bobbin pins," she said, giving each girl her share.

It was easy work and they soon had it done.

They watched Grandmother pin the pattern on the *mundillo*, a stuffed pillow held erect by a flat-board inside. The design on the cardboard pattern was carefully perforated. It had a fine scalloped border of marigolds on the edge. When she had it firmly pinned, she inserted a line of straight pins at the head of the pattern. On these she began to suspend the sixty-four bobbin pins the pattern called for. When she had them all adjusted evenly, she placed the *mundillo* on her lap, propped it against the beam holding the shed and began to work. She passed the bobbin pins over and under, weaving the thread along as she went, into the design represented on the pattern. Whenever she reached one of the perforations, she inserted a straight pin and wove in and out again, drawing the thread firmly about it. Little by little her fingers began to go faster until by the time she reached across the pattern, the sound of the bobbin pins resembled the clicking of castanets.

"Oh, Grandmother," said Mercedes, fascinated by the apparent ease with which she worked, "do you think I can learn how to make lace like that?"

"Anyone with patience and perseverance can learn. There are enough bobbin pins and patterns in the house which you can have. Teresa might as well learn, too."

Grandmother had begun to do the first petal of a marigold. Her weaving resembled a fine spider's web, she was so methodical and accurate, about the petal. When she finished it, she tied a wide band around the *mundillo* to keep the bobbin pins from tangling.

"If you really want to learn, have Ramón help you stuff two *mundillos*. You can start after dinner."

"Let's try to make our own patterns," said Teresa, after Grandmother had left. "It will be more fun."

They found Ramón whittling behind the woodshed and asked him to help them stuff the *mundillos*. When they finished, he brought the *mundillos* to the shed for them.

"Let me have the patterns and I'll pin them up for you," he said.

"We don't have them yet. We're going to make our own," Mercedes explained.

"Make your own patterns?" Ramón did not think they could really do them.

"You make designs for the things you carve, so why can't we make patterns for our lace?"

"Because it isn't the same thing. I don't have to figure out how many bobbin pins to a pattern, like you would have to."

"You are making it sound more difficult than it really is. We will show you when we have them ready," said Teresa.

First they made a design on a piece of paper. Teresa made one with a rose, and Mercedes one with a palm leaf. They looked at the pattern on Grandmother's *mundillo*. Besides the marigold, the pattern showed lots of perforations, which meant nothing to the girls, but they counted them to be sure to make the same on their pattern.

When they began to transfer their design to the cardboard, they realized the difficulty they were in. True, the rose and the palm leaf looked all right, but the rest of the perforations around them, which they had tried to copy from Grandmother's pattern, did not seem right. They went over them counting carefully, but with little success.

"Grandmother used sixty-four bobbin pins for her pattern," said Mercedes. "Evidently each perforation represents a bobbin pin, yet her pattern has lots more than sixty-four perforations. I can't figure it out. Can you, Teresa?"

Teresa's mouth was full of pins. She had been trying to solve the puzzle of her own pattern. Mercedes came to watch her work.

"Why, Teresa, your pattern is crooked. Look at it from this side and you'll see."

It was indeed crooked, so much so that the rose did not seem to belong to the rest of the intricate set of perforations with which she had surrounded it.

Teresa took the pins out of her mouth. "I give up," she said. "I have counted perforations and imaginary bobbin pins until I can't tell which is which."

"Let's show them to Grandmother," suggested Mercedes. "She can tell us what is wrong. If we cannot use them, there are still the patterns she has. Ramón was right after all."

Teresa did not like the idea at all, especially when she had boasted to Ramón, but what else could she do? She gathered up her work and followed Mercedes back to the house.

Ramón saw them leave the shed, dragging the *mundillo* along with them, and guessed the reason why.

"Make their own patterns," he said, giving the wood an extra cut. "I guess they found out."

When Grandmother saw them come in, she wondered what besides the *mundillos* the girls were bringing.

"They are patterns," Mercedes explained. "We tried to make our own."

One look at their work was sufficient to show Grandmother how hard both girls had struggled to put down their ideas. It took her time to convince them that no one could really attempt to do a pattern unless they knew how to make lace first. She brought out two of the simplest patterns and pinned them on their *mundillos*. When the girls wound the thread around the bobbin pins, she sat them near her and began to teach them the fundamental weaving, which was the base to all lace-making. Little by little their fingers began to feel less strained and more at ease, until they really began to enjoy the work. There were no frills to the pattern they worked from. Grandmother said that when they had made enough lace, they could use it on handkerchieves or petticoats.

Mercedes soon forgot the ruined pattern, but not Teresa. "Someday," she said, "I am going to make that pattern. Someday I shall know just how."

The girls worked till dinner time, and afterwards took their *mundillos* to their bedrooms where they continued to work long after the family had gone to bed.

Next morning, soon after breakfast, Grandmother saw them go downhill, carrying their *mundillos* along.

"Going to Sixta's," Teresa called back.

Grandmother was correct. With an inch of lace already reproduced on each pattern, the girls were as pleased as if they had a yard. Sixta would be surprised to see what they had done. Now they too could sit with her while she worked on her lace orders without feeling that they were in the way.

Sixta and her mother were pulling threads on an order of special-sized handkerchiefs for a house in Cayey. The girls stood their *mundillos* on chairs and untied the bands around the bobbin pins to show Sixta their work.

"It's the *entre dos* pattern, the one I like so much," Sixta said. "The one I made for your mother.

It's a beautiful pattern. You'll see the design much better when you have done a little bit more than what you have now."

"Did Grandmother lend you this pattern?" asked Mercedes.

"Yes, and many others." She left her work and returned with a pack of cardboard patterns. "They are all copies from Grandmother's patterns. I made them by placing a plain piece of cardboard under the original pattern and punching the perforations with this large pin. So now I don't have to be running up to ask for the loan of a pattern. I have my own."

"Have you ever made an original pattern?" asked Teresa.

"Heavens, no. I would not know how."

"But someone must have made the very first pattern," she insisted.

"That is true, but I do not have the least idea who it was, and what's more, I don't even care, not when you can always borrow patterns and copy the ones you like best."

"Grandmother said that when one knew how to make lace, one could make patterns."

"We tried to make some yesterday," said Mercedes, "even before we knew how to make lace. Wasn't that foolish?"

"I bet it was Teresa's idea," said Sixta.

"And not a very good one," said Teresa. "Yet, there must be some way to figure those patterns out. Someday I may even surprise you."

"In the meantime, be sure you make more than just that design. By the time you learn to do the others, you'll be glad to have ready-made patterns to work from."

"Here is the sample for the lace you are making," said Sixta's mother, unrolling a piece of lace out of a large roll.

"Oh, it is actually beautiful," Teresa said. "Sixta, have you made all the rest of the lace on that roll, too?"

"Those are my samples. I always leave a piece of everything I make. Sometimes I get special orders when I show them to the stores where I go applying for work."

She turned over one of the cardboard patterns. "I even keep the number of bobbin pins needed for each design marked on the back, so that I won't have to guess or run up to ask Grandmother."

She opened the rest of the samples. Some were as narrow as the one the girls were doing, others as wide as some of the crochet borders in Grandmother's sheets and pillow cases, and others were scalloped and filled with intricate designs.

"Do you still feel like making your own patterns, Teresa?" asked Sixta as the girls helped her roll up the samples again.

Teresa shook her head. "Not if I have to learn first how to do all of these patterns...but it was rather fun trying to yesterday. Today, I know better..."

# CHAPTER 8
# SHOPPING TRIP

Teresa, Ramón and Mercedes were out in the shed when Grandmother came with the long shears to work in her garden. Ramón picked up the pail of water and Teresa the watering can, and all three followed her.

The garden was on the south side of the house. It was a daily chore for Grandmother, taking hours of her time. Every summer Teresa had been her constant helper, but since Mercedes had come, Grandmother had been unable to enlist Teresa's help, for the two girls spent much of their free time walking about the *finca*. It had been Doña Anita who had solved the problem, by suggesting a definite day of the week to devote to the garden. That had saved arguments and time, and had given Grandmother three helpers instead of one.

"Look at those poor plants," Grandmother said, "What with the caterpillars, lizards and ants, it's a wonder there are any left. Start pulling those weeds, Teresa. Get Mercedes to help you. Ramón and I must start working on the other side."

As Grandmother approached a patch of flowering plants, she said, "Who would have thought that these geraniums would live, eh, Ramón? There are lots of new shoots up; I believe they are safe now." She turned over the earth about the plants.

Ramón tied the stalks of tuberoses which the wind had blown apart. The blooms were partly open, and the pungent scent filled the air. The carnation plants were full of buds. Some were beginning to open, showing their pink, white and deep red petals to the sun.

Grandmother's pride was a bed of pansies. It was a small one, but the plants yielded large saucy-faced pansies, soft and velvety to the touch. Butterflies as varied in hues as the pansies themselves hovered over the bed constantly.

"The sun has dried almost completely the border of *alhabaca*," said Teresa. "The stalks look like straw."

"Pick up the leaves then," said Grandmother. "They are just right to be used in the bay rum bottle."

Grandmother's bay rum bottle was a household possession. Into it went petals of roses and scented leaves from her garden.

The bottle had many uses. Sometimes it helped relieve Grandmother's aching back or stiff fingers or

Doña Anita's headaches. On extremely hot days, there was nothing more soothing than to mop one's forehead with a handkerchief soaked in the fragrant bay rum. Even Don Rodrigo used it on his face, like an after-shaving lotion, and said he preferred it to the lotions he bought at the drug store.

Close to some of the geranium plants, Ramón noticed a tiny sensitive plant. He touched it and watched the leaves fold up and close.

"Shall I pull it out, Grandmother? What good is a sensitive plant here?"

"No, let the *morivivi* be," she answered. "It will only grow up again."

The girls collected the dried leaves of the geranium and added them to the *alhabaca*. When Ramón brought the roses he had cut, they stuffed everything into the empty water can and then sat down to rest. Their backs ached from the stooping position they had been in all morning.

"I think we have done enough for one day," said Grandmother. "The sun is too hot to do anything else."

Gladly the girls picked up the watering can and followed her back to the house.

Doña Anita sat examining a fashion magazine and the girls joined her.

"When are we going to buy material for the dresses Sixta is going to make for us?" asked Teresa.

"With all the work lined up ahead of me, I can't tell when I can take you."

"You really don't have to take them shopping," said Grandmother. "Ramón is going to town tomorrow. Why not let the girls go along with him?"

Doña Anita hesitated for a minute, but finally agreed.

"Take Antonio along," Grandmother suggested. "He will never forgive you if you leave him behind."

The next day, Ramón was the first up and went to give Antonio the news. He shook Antonio's cot, but he did not awaken.

"Antonio," called his mother, giving the cot a shake that almost sent him to the bare floor. "Ramón is here and waiting for you."

"Ramón? Ramón?" he murmured half-asleep.

"Hurry up, Antonio," said Ramón. "We are going to Cayey and you are going with us."

Antonio sat up.

A trip to Cayey with Ramón, Teresa and Mercedes did not happen every day.

Teresa and Mercedes were waiting when the boys arrived.

Ramón saddled two horses: one for Mercedes and Teresa; the other for Antonio and himself. He put saddlebags on his own, for he had two pairs of heavy boots to bring back from town, besides the things Teresa was to buy.

"Ride along ahead, Ramón," said Don Rodrigo, "and let Teresa follow you. Stay close to the side of the road and look out for coaches."

Though it was early, the road was alive with farmers going to market. Some carried their vegetables on their backs, while others rode horses or pushed along large wheelbarrows.

"I can already see town," said Mercedes when the roofs of the first houses came into view.

"That is not the town," called back Antonio. "It's only the military headquarters."

"Wait, Ramón, let Mercedes see them," said Teresa, riding close to the gate. The American flag was being hoisted and soldiers stood at attention.

"No one ever goes in there," whispered Antonio, "unless they have a special pass. This is where the soldiers live."

"We also have soldiers in San Juan," said Mercedes. "They live in the Morro Castle and in the San Cristóbal Fort. No one goes there either, unless they have a pass."

"Come now," said Ramón, "you can look again when we come back."

As they drew away, tall American mules were brought from the stables. They had warm blankets over their backs. The children rode past the base and then their horses picked up speed. Soon they were crossing the small bridge into town. Ramón stopped at Martín's blacksmith shop at the entrance of town.

"Martín!" he called.

"*Buenos, buenos*," said Martín, coming out to greet him. "I see you brought company today."

Martín was the town blacksmith, loved by all the children of Cayey. His smithy shop was large and busy, yet never too busy to cater to the children who daily came to pick up the flat square slabs used in hopscotch games, but more often to see horses shod or watch the flaming piece of iron turn into shape under Martín's hard beating. During the course of the day, as Martín stood at the door of his shop, he saw many a pair of legs fly after one of the many rusty hoops he had given away.

Martín helped Ramón lead the horses to the stable. Teresa and Mercedes went into the smithy. The walls were lined with old harnesses and bridles; old broken coach wheels were piled in corners. There was a large anvil in the center of the room, and on one side, taking up a large portion of the wall, was the firebed.

"Aren't any horses coming to get shoes?" asked Antonio. "I would like to see it done."

"You do, eh?" said Martín. "Well, we will have to arrange for that."

Ramón started them on their way again, but not before Antonio had filled his pockets with flat slabs. They went up Comercio Street. The stores weren't open yet, so they walked to the public plaza.

"This is the town where father came to the meeting when he left me at the *finca*," said Mercedes. "I wonder where he stayed?"

"At the Hotel Comercio," said Ramón. "We are coming to it now. All meetings are always held there."

When they passed the hotel, the doors were closed. Evidently the guests were still in bed. Even the public square was deserted, except for one or two men sitting on benches.

"I am going to the church," said Antonio, running across the street. They followed him. Aside from a couple of old women saying their beads, the church, too, was deserted.

The sexton came out and began to refill the candle stands at each side of the railing. They watched him scrape out the old wax. He looked sleepy himself, yet managed to keep an eye on them. He had never seen children in church that early.

"How can he put the candles in the right place when his head is always turned watching us?" asked Mercedes.

The children sat down near the main altar. When the sexton finished placing the last candle, he opened the side door wide. Antonio, who stood near the door, caught sight of a large sign hanging from a door across the street. He spelled out the letters. "D-U-L-C-E-S"…"Candies!" he shouted.

"Hush," said Teresa.

But Antonio was already out of the church. They followed him to the candy shop. The door was closed and Ramón tried the knob. A bell sounded as the door opened and the children filed into the small shop. The place smelled of molasses, anise and peppermint. On the counter that stretched from side to side were platters filled with coconut, anise and raspberry drops. On a wooden rack were lollipops shaped and colored like farmyard animals.

"What are you doing here so early?" asked a man coming out of the kitchen.

"We are from the *finca*," said Antonio. "We came early to avoid the sun."

"A very good reason," remarked the man, now laughing. "What can I sell you?"

"I want three coconut drops and two peppermint sticks," said Teresa.

"I want anise drops," said Mercedes.

"Give me four raspberry ones," said Ramón.

Antonio moved from one side of the counter to the other, unable to decide what to have.

"Make up your mind, Antonio. You can't buy the entire shop. What would you have?" asked Ramón.

"Lollipops—all kinds," he said.

Teresa and Ramón let him pick the ones he wanted from the rack and paid the man.

"Wait a second, children," said the owner, going back to the kitchen. "I have just finished my birds," he said, putting on the counter a platter filled with the most colorful tiny birds imaginable.

"Oh!" cried the children, eager now to exchange their purchases for the colorful birds.

"I want that green parrot," said Antonio.

"And, I, that pigeon," said Mercedes.

The candymaker stood each bird on the counter as the children selected their favorites.

"Why don't you call for yours, too," he asked Ramón and Teresa. "They are my gifts to you."

They each took a robin and, thanking the man, left the shop.

When they came back to Comercio Street, the shops were open and the streets were full of people and stray dogs. The street vendors were everywhere calling their wares. "¡*Carbón*! ¡*Carbón*!" called the charcoal vendor. "Tomatoes—red tomatoes," called the vegetable men. "Buy my peppers and lettuce, señora," he called. He went from door to door peddling his wares.

The door of the small fruit store on the corner was filled with bunches of bananas hanging from its rafters. Inside, oranges, limes and grapefruits stood alongside mangoes and rich, red bananas. Piled on a large box were plantains, breadfruits, and a variety of tropical roots. Large platters of *achiote* seeds filled the counter and bags of all kinds of beans rested on the floor.

Soon they reached the department store. It was the biggest store in town and carried better merchandise than any of the others. Antonio and Ramón stood on the sidewalk while the girls did their shopping.

Teresa handed the clerk the list her mother had given her, and the clerk began to look for the things included on it.

"Anything else?" he asked when he had wrapped up buttons, pins, threads, tape and netting.

"Yes," said Teresa, "we want some material for dresses."

"Who are the dresses for?" asked the clerk.

"For us, of course," she answered. The clerk looked at the rolls of cloth on the shelves, selected four and put them on the counter. The girls looked them over.

"I like this one," said Mercedes, selecting a yellow organdy with embroidered rosebuds.

"I have always wanted to have a blue linen dress," said Teresa, deciding on a roll of cloth next to her. "We want two yards of each if it is forty-five inches wide or two-and-a-quarter, if it isn't. That's what Grandmother said."

The clerk nodded and began to measure the material.

"Please make out two separate packages." said Mercedes. "I would like to carry my own."

"Here you are," said the clerk. "Now that will be..."

"Oh, I almost forgot," said Teresa, handing him an envelope her father had given her.

"So you are Don Rodrigo's daughter," he said, looking for his ledger book, where he carefully entered the cost of the purchases.

When they came out Ramón and Antonio were glad to see them. They had waited a long time for them.

"Now for the shoemaker," said Ramón. They walked to the other side of town where the shoemaker's place was and picked the two pairs of heavy boots he had mended for Don Rodrigo. When they came back to the smithy, Martín was busy shoeing a horse.

"A horse!" cried Antonio, who refused to help Ramón bring the horses from the stable. He stood alongside Martín, watching as the shoemaker cleaned the horse's hoof, drew out the nails and lifted the old shoe. Not until he had seen how the new one was set did he move from the place. When they were ready to go, he pulled out one of his precious lollipops and gave it to Martín.

"Well, a rooster!" said Martín, "I will have to wait to eat it later, for I have much work to do right now."

Ramón paid Martín for the stable place and turned his horse towards the bridge and out on the road again.

Don Rodrigo, who had been on the lookout for them, saw them turn from the road and take the country road to the house.

"The children are back," he called, quite relieved now, for he had not liked the idea of letting them go alone on such a trip. Up the path the two horses came slowly, and soon stopped behind the house where the family had gathered to welcome the children back.

"How did the shopping go?" asked Grandmother, helping take the packages from the saddlebags. Don Rodrigo helped the children down, and Ramón and Antonio took the horses away.

"These are fine goods," said Doña Anita when the girls unwrapped the parcels. "I couldn't have done any better."

Don Rodrigo unwrapped his boots and examined the workmanship. He, too, was well satisfied. "They look just like new," he said.

"We bought something else," said Antonio, coming into the room. "Candy... all kinds."

He showed what was left of his purchase, which was not much, for he had been sucking lollipops since leaving.

A worker came in and handed Don Rodrigo a letter. "It's from Lucio," said Don Rodrigo.

"From *Papá!*" cried Mercedes enthusiastically.

"Is he coming back for Mercedes?" asked Teresa. "Summer is not over yet."

"Let us see what he has to say," said Don Rodrigo, tearing open the envelope and reading quickly. "Listen:

"'Dear Friend: Returning soon. Grand surprise.'"

"A surprise! A grand surprise!" cried the children. "What could it be?"

"A gift for everyone, perhaps," said Ramón. "He has been all over the island."

"Will he bring one for me, too?" asked Antonio.

"Don't make so much over Lucio's letter," said Grandmother. "God only knows what it is he's calling a surprise. Most likely a good business deal. Run along, Antonio, and stop eating candy. You will have nothing but empty sticks to show your mother."

The children were not the only ones excited over Lucio's news.

"What in the world can he mean by a grand surprise?" asked Don Rodrigo when Teresa and Mercedes had gone to their room.

"Let us wait and see," said his wife. "You sound worse than the children.

# CHAPTER 9
# FIESTA

The next day, the girls took their material to Sixta, but the novelty of the news Lucio had sent had worn off the excitement of the new dresses.

"I could hardly sleep," said Mercedes. "All night I did nothing but turn and turn, and wonder what the surprise would be. Who do you think it's for, Teresa?"

"Hope it is for Ramón, as I am hoping."

"But why for Ramón, especially?"

"Because it might be news about his family."

"What else is there to know about his family?" said Mercedes. "He knows his parents died long ago. Your father has even tried to find relatives, without any success. I don't understand what you mean, Teresa."

"Exactly what you have just said. There might be other relatives that we don't know about. Ramón and I are always hoping some letter will bring him more news someday. That's why I hope Lucio's surprise might be for him. And you too would hope it would be, if you had lost your parents and didn't even know who they were. Just think how happy Ramón would be if he actually found out the real story about them."

Mercedes kept quiet. She just did not know what to answer. Teresa was right about her hopes, but she had the right to hope for anything else she wanted. If in sixteen years no relatives had ever shown up to claim Ramón, she did not think he had any. Everyone in Cayey and Cidra knew Don Rodrigo and the story about Ramón. It would have been easy to find his relatives if there had been any. No, she was not wasting her hopes on that.

When they reached Sixta's house, they told her about Lucio's letter even before they displayed the goods for her to see.

"Don't plan too much," said Sixta. "It's better to wait without too much planning. Then the surprise will turn out to be a real one."

The girls opened their packages and spread the material for her to see.

"What fine organdy, and what a soft shade of blue linen." Sixta was pleased. She knew she would enjoy turning such material into dresses.

"How are you going to make them? Did you see the fashion magazine I sent Doña Anita? There are two pages of dresses you might like to choose from."

"We want them alike," said Teresa.

"But you can't have them alike," Sixta explained. "The materials are so very different." She thought for a while.

"I have an idea," Sixta said. "If you like, I can have these dresses ready for you soon. This blue material will be just right for a princess-style dress, with a square neck and buttons from top to bottom. I can make the sleeves scalloped and embroider the edges." There was enthusiasm in Sixta's voice. She liked nothing better than to follow her own ideas when sewing.

"Now, Mercedes' organdy can be made into a dress with two ruffles at the bottom. There is enough material here for even a sash. What do you think, girls?"

They did not look very happy about Sixta's plans. Sixta realized that the girls had not understood the description of the dress she had given

So, she drew two pictures on a piece of paper to illustrate her point.

The change that came over the girls' faces satisfied her.

"It was foolish of us to want two identical dresses, as if we were twins," said Mercedes, laughing. "I like mine just like this picture."

"Me, too," said Teresa.

Sixta took their measurements before they left and told them she would let them know when to come back for a fitting.

When Teresa and Mercedes returned home, they took their *mundillos* out to the shed. Both had gained speed and were really enjoying their lace-making.

"There's Pilar coming up the hill," said Mercedes.

"Ho, Pilar!" called Teresa.

Pilar waved to them on her way to the house. She stopped by the kitchen to speak with Lucía, then asked to see Doña Anita or Grandmother.

They were surprised to hear about her call, for Pilar did not come often to the house. If she was here, she must have a reason...a special reason.

"It's nice to see you," said Grandmother, offering her a chair.

Pilar took out a letter from the pocket of her skirt and handed it to Doña Anita. "Felipe and I thought you ought to see this," she said.

"A birthday *trulla*! Why, Pilar, there has not been a *trulla* on this *finca* for years. Felipe is lucky to have his friends remember his birthday in this way. *Trullas* are omens of merrymaking...and luck for the household where they come. Is there anything we can do to help?"

Pilar hesitated for a moment. Her request was an unusual one, and she did not know how it would be received.

Grandmother noticed her hesitation and wondered what could be on her mind. Wasn't she happy about the *trulla*?

"What is it, Pilar?" she asked.

"There will be some children coming," said Pilar, "and I thought Mercedes and Teresa might like to meet them and stay to see the *trulla*. I will look after them and see that they get home safely."

That had been the last thing they expected from Pilar, and Grandmother began to laugh.

"I thought for a while you really did not want the *trulla* to come, Pilar, and you did not know how to get out of it. I'm glad it was not that," said Grandmother.

"Try and keep those two away from anything going on in the *finca*," said Doña Anita. "That is your first wish for the *trulla*, and it is granted. Ramón will bring them in time to see the feast from beginning to end."

"*Gracias*, Doña Anita," said Pilar. "The girls are in the shed. Will it be all right to tell them?"

"Not until I tell her father first, Pilar," said Doña Anita.

Pilar rose to go. She hoped Don Rodrigo, too, would consent to let the girls participate.

"Wait a minute, Pilar," said Grandmother. She left the room and soon returned with a small envelope. "For the *trulla*," she said, slipping it into Pilar's hands.

Down the road, before she reached her house, Pilar opened the envelope. Folded neatly inside were eight one-dollar bills. Eight one-dollar bills and all for a *trulla*! But wouldn't that be extravagance? There were so many things they could do with that extra money.

There was that trip to San Juan Felipe had promised her and the feast of Candelamas Day in the highlands of Guayama—she would like to see that. Then, there was Ponce. Valentín was always talking about Ponce, with its Vigía and its two public plazas. "¡*Ay!*" She would like to see all those things someday.

Last year she had heard Grandmother tell about the hot springs in Coamo. Did Grandmother mean real hot water out of the earth? Even that would be worth seeing.

After dinner, when she had washed her dishes, swept her kitchen and hung up her apron, Pilar went to sit near her husband, who was smoking his cigar outside the door. She told him about her visit to Doña Anita's home and gave him Grandmother's gift. "It's for the *trulla*," she said, secretly hoping he would let her keep it.

But her husband had his own ideas about his gift. Pictures of all the rich food he had always wanted and could not afford rose in his mind.

"Let's have a real feast for once, Pilar," he said. "This is our money...money we have not worked for...a real gift."

He enumerated the things he could buy with it. Chickens, olives and capers for the *arroz con pollo*. He could see his plate garnished with thick slices of *pimientos morrones*—the tasty Spanish peppers— and sprinkled with green peas. He swallowed hard. Then there were *pasteles* and almonds, even marzipan for dessert. He went on and on.

Pilar listened quietly as in his mind he went spending not only the eight dollars but three times the amount.

He re-read the letter. "Fifteen people, that's splendid," he said. "Even Don Goyo is coming. Time is short, Pilar. Better ask some of your friends to give you a hand in the kitchen while I get Gregorio and Valentín to help me lay a floor in the rear of the house. If Don Goyo is coming, there is bound to be music, and if there is music, there will be dancing."

On Friday morning, five of Pilar's friends came to help her. Each brought a gift: green plantains, papayas, tomatoes, onions and casaba bread. When Valentín and Gregorio arrived, they brought three large breadfruits, six dry coconuts and a bowl of dry ginger roots.

Pilar was pleased. "Come and see your presents, Felipe," she called.

"It's nothing much," said their friends, "but we wanted to help you celebrate. A *trulla* is a *trulla*."

As they stood sorting the gifts, a sharp whistle ran through the air. They listened.

Only one person whistles like that, thought Felipe.

The whistle came again…long…sharper than before. Yes, there was no doubt now: It must be Martín. He ran to the door.

Martín was making his way up the hill. He was so fat that he had to walk slowly. Over his shoulder he carried a string of chickens tied together by their legs.

"What is a *trulla* without *arroz con pollo*?" he said as he reached the house. "I could not wait for the oxcart, so I came ahead."

He walked to the kitchen, threw his load on the table and dropped on a bench, puffing out his breath. "This hill and I are enemies, Pilar," he said, laughing.

"Is anybody around?" said a voice at the door.

It was Ramón, and he, too, had brought a present for Felipe. "From Doña Anita," he said, putting a kettle on the table.

Before Pilar had removed the cover, a savory smell rose from it.

"Ground beef!" said Pilar, sniffing.

"Of course," said Martín. "Ground beef cooked with olives and capers, tomatoes and peppers—just the thing for *pasteles*. Whoever heard of a *trulla* without *pasteles*, Pilar?"

Never had Pilar seen so many gifts in her house before. If *trullas* brought such things, why didn't they come more often?

"Why, we have everything for the *trulla* now, Felipe," she said. Her mind was on the eight dollar bills. She was positive they did not have to spend it. There were other things in the house that she could add to the gifts.

Her husband must have read her thoughts, for he dug into his pocket, brought out Grandmother's gift and handed it to her. The *trulla* had even worked its magic spell over her husband. Eight dollar bills now safe in her pocket!

"Clear the kitchen," she said gladly. "We have work to do."

Felipe took his friends outside to help build the dancing floor, while Pilar and her friends settled down to work. Soon they had the green plantains peeled and grated for the *pasteles*—the Puerto Rican tamales. The papayas were sliced and boiling with sugar and bars of cinnamon, the coconuts grated for *manpostiales*. Only the *arroz con pollo* remained to be cooked and that was never done beforehand.

Ramón cut banana leaves to wrap the *pasteles* in before they were set to boil, and even helped Pilar hold them over the fire to make them supple.

When the men finished their work, Pilar brewed some coffee and gave each a cup. They sat in the kitchen talking about the *trulla* until they were ready to go. Only Martín remained to spend the evening with Pilar and Felipe.

Saturday morning, the day of the *trulla*, the rules and regulations at Don Rodrigo's home were forgotten. The girls even took a holiday from the stockroom. Their minds were on the *trulla*, and nothing else mattered to them.

"A whole day at a *trulla*," said Teresa, her eyes sparkling in anticipation of all she was going to see. "Mother said Don Goyo was coming. Wait until you see him! What songs he sings! What stories he tells!"

"Why can't we leave now?" asked Mercedes, who had never seen a birthday *trulla* and was tired of waiting.

"Because no one ever arrives before the *trulla*. A birthday *trulla* is different from a Christmas one." Mercedes knew about those. They came from Christmas Eve right on until Three Kings Day, on January the 6th. They went from house to house singing carols, dancing and eating all the sweets they were served.

Ramón and Antonio had gone down the road to watch for the *trulla*.

Almost as Teresa finished talking, Antonio came running into the room shouting, "It's coming, it's coming!"

"Come along, Mercedes," said Teresa, running out of the house. "The *trulla* is here at last."

A large oxcart trimmed with branches and full of people was coming along the road. They could see it clearly as they ran down hill. There were five children: three girls about Mercedes' age and two boys as young as Antonio. In their midst sat Don Goyo. The cart came to a stop as the girls reached the road.

"Everybody out," shouted the driver. "I'll meet you back here after the fiesta."

"We are going to Felipe's home, too," said Ramón, "and have been waiting for you to arrive so that we could all go together."

"Just the thing," said Don Goyo. "You can lead the way. The cart will have to stay down here until we return."

Don Goyo shook hands with Teresa and, after inquiring about her father, introduced the group of children who stood around him.

Ramón took a shortcut to the house and soon brought them to Felipe's house.

"What would *fincas* be without shortcuts?" Don Goyo said as the group stood facing the house.

The door was closed. It was difficult to believe that inside Felipe and Pilar were eagerly waiting, with tables and pots and pans full of good things to eat.

Don Goyo assembled his group. One of the girls came forward with a bouquet of flowers. Then the musicians, with their native instruments, surrounded her. The rest of the group stood behind them.

"Now," said Don Goyo, waving his hand like a conductor. The musicians struck a chord and the group began to sing. When they finished, Don Goyo knocked at the door. Immediately, the door opened and Felipe and Pilar came out smiling to greet them. A young girl presented a bouquet of flowers to Pilar, who, joining hands with her husband, raised them forming an arch.

"The arch is made. Welcome all to my birthday party," said Felipe.

Only after such simple formalities did the guests go into the house one after the other. Pilar led the children to the table, where small gourds filled with coconut and papaya candy had been set aside for them.

Then Martín offered a toast to Felipe's health and the success of the *trulla*.

They all sat on benches and chairs borrowed from their friends while Pilar passed them some of the candy she had reserved for them. The children stood around the table eating until Ramón signaled them to follow him outside.

The musicians came out, too, and laid their instruments on the floor.

"What, no music?" said Gregorio, who had followed them. "Play, *amigos*, play. Let us start this *trulla* in the proper fashion."

The musicians picked up their instruments and struck a series of chords. At the sound of them the rest of the guests came out.

"Partners get ready," called Don Goyo, "the *seis* is about to begin."

This was the most popular peasant dance, and the favorite at all *trullas*.

"Come, Mercedes," said Teresa. She made her way through the group of adults. "It's no fun to see the dance from a distance when we can stand in front of the dancing floor."

Don Goyo took his special seat and clapped his hands. Six couples took their places on the floor, forming two straight lines, so that the men came to be facing the women. The music began, and the dancers started tapping their feet. They intersected each other, swaying to the rhythm of the music. At the next call from Don Goyo, the partners came together and waltzed around the floor. On and on they waltzed until his call came again. The couples now turned back to back and danced away. Every now and then the men looked over their shoulders at their retreating partners, who disdainfully tossed their heads and danced away from them.

The group of spectators clapped their hands and shouted to the couples, encouraging them with their remarks.

Twice around the dancing floor the couples went, the women tossing their heads to the rhythm of the *seis*, followed by their partners, who were trying to regain their graces. Don Goyo called once more, and the couples came together again. The music changed to a faster tempo, and the couples whirled furiously about the room.

"*Bomba*," called Don Goyo. The music ceased and the couples stopped dancing.

"Is it over?" asked Mercedes.

"No, no," said Gregorio. "This is only a short rest period. Then the *bombas* will begin."

"What are *bombas*?" she whispered to Teresa.

"A four-line poem each couple has to improvise when they are called upon," Teresa explained.

Now the couples were getting into a ring. They had scarcely finished when Don Goyo called, "*Bomba*, Valentín and Eusebia."

The couple stood in the center of the ring and began to sing until the *bomba* was finished.

A loud burst of applause rose from the group.

The music began again and the couples resumed their dancing until Don Goyo called another couple for their *bomba*.

"How can they think so fast," said Ramón, watching the couples swing into the dance, then stop, sing their improvised *bomba* and continue to dance.

Almost every couple had been called, when Pilar came to the kitchen door and called, "*Arroz con pollo.*" That put an end to the *seis*. The musicians put their instruments down and the couples left the floor. They followed Felipe to the kitchen, where platters of steaming *pasteles* and *arroz con pollo* awaited all.

The children bounced into the room and took the chairs closest to the table.

After Pilar served them, Ramón took them outside again.

"Let's sit on the dance floor," said one of the children.

Pilar brought them a pitcher of lemonade and some glasses. When they finished eating, some of the children began to run over the floor, imitating the dance they had seen. Ramón and Teresa urged the children on, who now outdid themselves to please their audience. They hummed whatever they remembered of the music, skipping over the floor in their effort to make their steps as similar as possible to the ones they had watched the couples do.

"How would you like to see some of the *finca*?" asked Teresa.

Ramón stood up ready to lead them. The children jumped off the floor eager to follow him.

"All plates and glasses back to the kitchen first," said Ramón.

When they returned, he led them past the cistern and down the hill.

"Almond trees! Almonds," cried the children, scattering to pick up the dried nuts that covered the ground. They looked for sharp stones to crack them open.

"The public plaza at home is lined with almond trees," said one of the boys.

"If you eat nuts with bread, they taste like coconuts," said one of the girls to Mercedes. "Have you ever eaten them?"

"No, but I know something else that tastes like coconut when you eat it with bread."

"What?" she asked.

"Avocados. I have tried that."

"I think the nuts in Arroyo taste different," said Teresa. "Grandmother says that it is the sea that makes them salty. I ate some there once."

"You have eaten enough," said Ramón. "Let's go now."

The children stuffed their pockets and shirts with nuts, and then followed him.

When they came to the river and the children spotted the flat stones, they took off their shoes and waded in. They stood upon the stones, splashing water on each other until their clothes were soaked.

"Come off those stones," cried Teresa, afraid the children might slip off. But the children's shouts drowned out her voice.

Ramón and Mercedes ran along the edge, trying to call Antonio, who had also joined the rest of the children.

At last, they jumped off and sat on the grass, laughing, water dripping from their clothes.

"Don't take them to the pool," whispered Teresa to Ramón. "They will all want to go swimming. Let's show them the tobacco sheds instead."

They turned off the river path and crossed the field out to the tobacco plots. By the time they reached the first shed, the sun had dried their clothes. Most of the children knew about sugar cane plantations, but they had never been on a tobacco plantation. So Ramón and Teresa took turns telling them about it.

"Where is the tobacco?" asked one of the boys.

"There's none here now, but this is the place where the bunches of leaves are dried when they come from the fields."

"Where do they make the cigars?" asked one of the girls.

"Cigars?" asked Antonio, surprised at her question.

"This is a tobacco *finca*, isn't it?" she asked, tossing her head at Antonio.

"Of course," he answered, "but it is not a tobacco store like the ones in Cayey, where the men sit all day making cigars."

They left the tobacco shed and went by the end of a cow path, up the hill and back to the house.

The group was sitting under the trees and Pilar was singing. When she finished, Felipe said, "Now, Don Goyo, on with your yarn, and make it as good as you've ever told."

The children surrounded him.

Don Goyo buried the stub of his cigar in the ground and cleared his throat.

"Have you ever heard the story of 'The Pirate's Ghost'?" he asked.

"No," said the crowd. "That sounds good. Tell it, please."

"Once upon a time," said Don Goyo, "there was a village by the sea whose inhabitants were the most superstitious people in the entire world. They were fishermen by trade and worked diligently all days during the week, except Fridays. They had a firm belief that on Fridays evil forces were at work. And if you allowed yourself to be caught by them, nothing but evil was in store for you. So they stayed in their homes, and the entire place looked like a deserted village.

"Now one day, there came to the village a man called Pablo. He was short and stocky, but what he lacked in height he made up in strength and courage—not to mention his wits, which had saved him from many a scrape. He had not been there long before the villagers tried to intimidate him with the superstitious tales they loved to tell. To their surprise, Pablo only laughed and refused to believe them. His behavior angered the villagers, who began to eye him with distrust. They did everything to show him what an intruder they considered him to be.

"To prove how wrong they were, Pablo bought a fishing boat and a pair of fish nets one Friday afternoon. While the villagers were safe in their homes behind locked doors, he pushed off to sea. He sailed on and on until, looking back, the village seemed to be a speck in the distance. After hours of sailing, he reached an inlet surrounded by high coral reefs. Beyond them was the shore outlined by palm trees growing so close that they resembled a dense forest.

"Pablo cast his first net. Immediately, it filled to the brim with silvery fish. He pulled it in and cast out the second. No sooner had it touched the water, when it, too, filled up. He was about to pull it up when a strong gust of wind almost threw him off balance. The sky darkened and a thin rain began to fall. Pablo tried to steer his boat and turn it towards home, but the force of the wind turned it in the opposite direction. It now raced over the waves as if steered by a strange power. Nearer and nearer to the reefs it came. Pablo took one look at the sharp pointed edges and, summoning all his courage, jumped overboard. The empty boat continued to race straight ahead and crashed between the reefs, sending the fish back to the bottom of the sea.

"Struggling to keep above water, Pablo managed to swim away. How long he swam and how he finally found himself nearing the shore, he never knew, but that mattered little to him when he finally felt his feet touch bottom. He dragged himself to the beach and, making his way between the palm trees, arrived at a small clearing. He sat down to rest. He had scarcely closed his eyes when he felt the weight of a hand upon his shoulders.

"'¡*Caracoles*! What was that?' he shouted, jumping to his feet.

"Lo and behold, there in front of him stood the strangest-looking specimen of a man, or his ghost, that he had ever come in contact with. The man was tall, and his thin body was covered by a tattered pirate suit. His shaggy hair reached his shoulders, and a pair of gold loops dangled from his ears. In one hand he carried a spade; in the other a lighted torch.

"Pablo's courage left him, and his legs began to shake. 'This is the pirate's ghost, the sentry of the Devil's Hole!' he muttered.

"The very ghost the villagers fear so much... and now here it was right in front of him.

"Before another thought crossed his mind, he heard the pirate say, 'Take this torch in your right hand, cross the left over your shoulder and follow me.'"

"Like one under a magic spell, Pablo obeyed.

"Then a strange thing happened. The minute his hand touched the torch, a sense of adventure seized him and he felt his courage coming back. He followed the pirate on and on, across the clearing and still further beyond. When they reached another clearing, the pirate ordered him to stop. He drew a circle around Pablo and began to jump and stamp his feet, muttering strange words. Three times he went around him and then dropped to his knees and began to dig. He dug until a high pile of earth rose at his side. A rusty chain appeared. He tugged and tugged at it until the pile of chain equaled the height of the pile of earth. Finally, a small square chest appeared dangling at the end of the last bit of chain. With an eerie shout of triumph, the pirate pounced upon it and pried the lid open.

"The brightness that came from it dazzled Pablo's eyes. Never had he seen such splendor. Rubies, emeralds, diamonds and other precious stones difficult for him to identify lay alongside gold doubloons.

"The pirate looked frantically through the precious stones, lifting one handful after another and examining them carefully.

"'What could he be looking for?' thought Pablo.

"Then he saw what it was. Out of the last handful of gems, the pirate had taken a miniature dagger encased in a scabbard studded with tiny diamonds, sapphires and pearls. As soon as he laid eyes on it, Pablo felt a strange desire. He must have that dagger, even if he had to fight the pirate for possession.

"Pablo took one step forward. The pirate was examining the dagger closely, and his eyes gleamed. Pablo took another step and leaped, but his feet tangled on the pile of chain and he fell. The light of the torch went out.

"'The light! The light!' screamed the pirate. 'What have you done with the light, miserable fool?'

"A great rumbling noise rose from the earth, and a cold wind blew, chilling Pablo's very bones. When he finally picked himself up, the pirate's ghost had disappeared. On the spot where he had stood, Pablo saw something gleaming and shining as bright as the stars in the sky on a dark night.

"'It's the dagger!' he cried, rushing towards it. He stumbled over something else.

"'¡Caracoles! ¡Caracoles!' he shouted joyfully. 'The chest! The pirate left his treasure behind.'

"The next morning, when the first gleam of daylight brightened the sky, Pablo covered his loot with leaves and carried it carefully through the palm trees until he reached a town. There he bought a boat and returned to his village.

"Not a word did he say about his past experiences in the Devil's Hole. In fact, he could not have told them had he cared to, for when the villagers saw him, they ran away from him as one would from a wild beast. Even the children peered at him from behind their mother's skirts with fear in their eyes.

"So on the following Friday, Pablo picked up his belongings and sailed away. He settled in another village, where he bought himself a fine house, filled it with servants and took to live the life of a grand *señor*.

"Meanwhile in the village, Pablo's second disappearance struck a vital note. It was clear now to them that he was linked with evil forces. Before long, they had a yarn which reached mysterious proportions with each retelling, a yarn as strange and as worthy of these people who, as I told you before, were the most superstitious people in the entire world.'"

Don Goyo got to his feet as his audience burst into applause.

"We better move on," he said. "It is not so good to travel at night in an oxcart."

Mercedes, Teresa and Ramón said goodbye and thanked Pilar and Felipe for the good time they had had.

"Wait for us," said Don Goyo. "We can all walk together."

They went down the hill, still discussing Pablo's good luck.

The driver harnessed the oxen to the cart, and the children jumped into their seats.

"Goodbye, goodbye," they called as the cart began to move.

Ramón, Teresa and Mercedes stood waving to them until the trees hid them from view.

As the trio turned towards home, the wind brought back the sound of the voices of the children singing in the oxcart.

# CHAPTER 10
# 26 TAMARINDO

The day after the birthday *trulla*, Teresa and Mercedes entertained the family with their accounts of the celebration. They even went through some of the steps of the *seis*.

"I see Don Goyo preserves the original form of the dance," Don Rodrigo said, watching the girls go whirling around the room.

"Do you know that this *seis* used to be an old ritual of the church and was first danced by little children with their heads uncovered during the feast of Corpus Christi?" said Grandmother.

"I always go to the feast at the small chapel on Cristo Street," said Mercedes, "but never have I seen children dance there."

"Of course not," said Grandmother. "This happened in the old days, and the custom has been abandoned. No one dances the *seises* for religious purposes anymore. At present, the only form seen here is the popularized *seis* which has come to be a set piece at all peasant dances. It's always the last piece the musicians play to end the dance."

"Let's end ours with it, too," said Don Rodrigo, laughing. "If we don't get to the *finca* and see about those six new sheds, they will never be finished. Come on, Ramón."

"How about sewing the sachets this morning, *Mamá*?" asked Doña Anita. "I have enough material in the basket now."

"That's a good idea," said Grandmother, following her daughter out of the room.

Teresa and Mercedes looked out the window. Ramón had brought the two horses and was waiting for Don Rodrigo to come out.

"How long will it be before you let me see the sandalwood box Ramón gave you, Teresa? You promised that if I ever came to the *finca*, you would show it to me. But every time I remind you, there is something else you want to do. Don't you really want to show it to me?"

"I guess I have to," she said, watching Ramón and her father ride away. "A promise is a promise. Let's go back to my room."

Out of an old trunk from under the window, Teresa took out a small bundle wrapped up in one of her father's handkerchieves. She untied the knots and showed Mercedes a small sandalwood box.

"I have not opened this box since Ramón gave it to me," she said, removing the lid carefully so that Mercedes could see its contents.

The box was neatly lined inside. Wound round and round a small cushion was a coral necklace and a pair of matching earrings.

"Oh, Teresa, it's so beautiful!" said Mercedes. "How long is it?"

Teresa did not really know.

"Haven't you ever worn it?"

"I have never taken it out of this box. I want to keep it as carefully as Ramón had himself. You see, he believes it once belonged to his mother."

"Let me see how it looks on me."

Before Teresa could stop her, she had taken out the necklace, slipped it over her head and gone to look at herself in the mirror.

"Look how long it is, Teresa. It has gone twice around my neck."

Mercedes turned around for her to see, but Teresa was busy examining something close by the window.

"What is it?" asked Mercedes.

"This tiny, crumpled card fell out of the sandalwood box when you took out the necklace," she said. "Here is the mark under the cushion where it had been."

"Let me see it," said Mercedes.

It was a wrinkled card, yellow with age. There was something written on it, which Teresa had been trying to make out. They smoothed the card out and together tried to decipher the writing.

"There is an R and an A," said Mercedes, "but the others are so creased that I can't read them."

"They look like an N and another A," said Teresa.

"Let's write the letters down on paper, so we can make out what they mean."

They substituted dots for the empty spaces.

"RA...NA—what do you suppose it means, Mercedes?"

"Look, Teresa, here is a capital A as clear as it can be, and isn't that a Y?"

"It is," said Teresa, "but the rest is missing, too, except for those two others which look like an L and another A." She put them down beside the ones she had written. They made out "AY...LA."

"This is a name, I am sure," said Mercedes.

Teresa put the card down and concentrated on the slip of paper.

"Let's substitute the letters of the alphabet, until we get some name out of it," said Mercedes.

Some of the letters made little sense, until they came to the M and the N.

"RAMONA!" cried the two excited girls.

They began to work with the second name. As soon as they added the first letter of the alphabet, they made out "AYALA."

"There it is complete now: 'RAMONA AYALA.' You were right, Mercedes. It is a name. Perhaps it is Ramón's mother's name."

She picked up the card and inserted the missing letters in their proper places.

"There's something written on the back of the card, too," said Mercedes. "Turn it over and see."

On a side that had escaped the creases was written 26 Had.

"What do you suppose it all means, Teresa?"

"I don't know for sure, but that is what you and I will have to find out. Only, we mustn't tell anyone until we know. Not even Ramón. Will you promise?"

"Of course," said Mercedes, "but how are we going to find out if we don't tell someone?"

"We can, we can," Teresa assured her, "if we find where 26 Tamarindo is. It must be the name of a street."

"But we are always at the *finca*. How are we to find out?"

"By asking, of course. Let me have the necklace back." She wound it around the cushion again, closed the box, wrapped it in the handkerchief and put it back in the trunk.

When they came back to the front room, Grandmother said she was just about to call them to help fill the sachets with dried patchouli. She gave them a handful of sachets she had finished sewing.

The girls sat down to work with their minds full of the secret they were keeping between them.

"If Teresa thinks of asking where 26 Tamarindo is, why does not she begin now?" thought Mercedes. She looked at her friend, but Teresa was working, apparently interested in the work she was doing.

Maybe if she began, she could give Teresa a lead to ask Grandmother. She could try anyhow. So she asked Grandmother why the paths in the *finca* did not have names.

"What an idea," said Grandmother. "There aren't that many."

"But for the few there are, there could be names," Mercedes insisted. "There is the path leading to the butterflies. Why can't it be called Butterfly Path?" She was carried away by her sudden idea.

"Oh, Teresa," she said, "let's make a map of the *finca* and name the places we like best."

"There is a map of the *finca*," said Doña Anita. "Hasn't Teresa shown it to you? Rodrigo has all the important places marked with red ink."

"I wonder if the place where the big tamarind tree is has been marked?" asked Teresa. "I don't remember."

Mercedes looked at her quickly. Teresa smiled. She had gotten her point after all.

"I don't remember it either," said her mother.

"Tamarind is a good name even for a street, isn't it, Grandmother?" asked Mercedes, for whom the conversation had taken an added interest now that Teresa was with her.

"Someone else must have thought the same thing," Grandmother said, "because there are some streets by that name."

"There are? Where?" both girls asked, forgetting all cautiousness.

"Isn't there one in Cidra, next to the public square?" asked Doña Anita.

"No," said Grandmother, "that is Tuna Street, but there is one in Cayey."

Antonio's arrival interrupted the conversation. Sixta had sent him to fetch Teresa and Mercedes to go and try on the new dresses.

The girls followed Antonio quickly out of the house. They were glad to see him turned towards his home, leaving them to go alone to Sixta's house.

"We must go to Cayey and find out," said Teresa, as soon as Antonio was gone.

"Maybe Ramón will take us again," said Mercedes.

"No, not Ramón, Mercedes, I don't want him to know why we want to go there."

"How about Sixta? She has to return some of her work sometime."

"That's it, Mercedes. Sixta, of course. Why didn't I think of her before."

They ran the rest of the way until they reached Sixta's house.

"I did not expect you so soon," said Sixta when they arrived. "Antonio must have misunderstood me. I said you could come down any day except Thursday. That is the day when I go to deliver my work in Cayey and pick a new batch."

"Can we go along with you?" asked Teresa.

"But I go on business and come right back. It won't be any fun for you."

"We can always walk around town while you deliver your work, and meet you at Martín's place."

"Please take us," said Teresa. "Mother will let us go if you come and ask her."

"All right," said Sixta. "Let's get on with these dresses, since you are here now. I think I can have them ready for you by the end of the week."

Sixta adjusted the seams and took up the hem of both dresses while the girls stood up on chairs. But they showed little interest in the dresses. Teresa wished she could tell Sixta about their plan, but she had decided not to let anyone know. Maybe after they looked for 26 Tamarindo, but not before.

Sixta kept her promise, and on Thursday Teresa and Mercedes led their horse towards the road where Sixta was already waiting. They carried the basket of lunch Grandmother had prepared. Concealed under it was the sandalwood box.

Sixta was also carrying a basket filled with her work.

"What's in your basket?" Sixta asked when the girls joined her.

"Lunch," said Teresa. "Grandmother thought we might stop on the way back and eat it in some cool place, like we were out on a picnic."

"I might have known it was a picnic you were thinking of all the time. But, since we have to eat somewhere, we might as well do it under the trees instead of in a hot, stuffy restaurant in town."

Sixta was a good rider and the girls found it hard to keep up with her.

When they reached the smithy, Martín was standing at the door talking to a group of men.

"Wo!" he called gladly. "The *finca* has come to town." He looked up the road, expecting to see another horse.

"No, Martín, Ramón and Antonio stayed home this time," said Teresa.

He helped them down and took their horses away. When he returned, Sixta was gone and Teresa had taken the sandalwood box from the bottom of the basket.

"Will you keep this lunch for us, Martín? We are coming back here to meet Sixta after she delivers her work and picks up the new orders."

"And where are you bound?" he asked. "Is it the candy shop again?"

"No, Martín, but to Tamarindo Street. How far is it from here?"

"Now, let me see. I have not been in that part of town for some time." He thought for a while and then gave them some directions. "Go up Comercio Street," he said, "until you come to Palma, then turn left and walk three blocks, then turn right. Yes, I think that is correct."

He stood at the door, basket in hand, watching them run up the street. "Whatever's taking them to that street must be important," he said to himself, "running that way and the heat of the sun rising." Martín sighed. Many a time he, too, had raced up that street, but that had been many years ago. He looked for the coolest place in his shop to set down the lunch basket.

When the girls reached Palma Street, it seemed to them as if they had crossed the full length of the town. It was a narrow street shaded by high trees. The wooden houses stood close together on each side of the street. There was no sidewalk, so the girls walked in the middle of the street, dodging wheelbarrows, cats and scrawny-looking dogs, besides children and grownups who seemed to be out sunning themselves.

They turned left and walked three blocks. They came into the shortest street they had ever seen. Almost in front of them was a pole with a placard across it. Tamarindo Street they read on it, and the first house they came to had a number six written out in black letters.

"It's on this side of the street," said Teresa. "Let's walk close to the houses—the numbers are not very clear."

They checked each house, because in some of them the paint was cracked and the numbers were even missing.

At last they came to a large square house with a backyard full of trees. The girls stopped. Right on the door was a large 26.

"26 Tamarindo, at last! I wonder what is behind that door for us," said Teresa.

"We will never know if we stand here just looking," said Mercedes.

They knocked.

"*Entre*—come in," said a voice.

They pushed the door and went in.

The room was filled with stools facing a large blackboard with the first six letters of the alphabet legibly written out in yellow and white chalk. Two middle-aged women sat on black rocking chairs, embroidering.

"*Buenos días*," said Teresa. "We would like to see Ramona Ayala."

The two women jumped to their feet. "What is that you said?" they asked.

Teresa repeated her question. "We have a card with her name and address in this box," she continued, untying the handkerchief.

"The coral necklace! How did you come by this box, children?" they asked.

It did not take Teresa long to explain how it had come to her house and had become her possession, and how through Mercedes' curiosity she had found the yellow creased card.

"We want to see Ramona," said Mercedes when Teresa finished.

"You have come to the right place," said one of the women. "However, Ramona had been dead for many years."

"Dead?" the girls exclaimed. "Then we have made the trip in vain."

"We are the sole survivors of the Ayala family," she continued, ignoring their remark. "I am Gloria, and this is my sister, Selina. We both recognized the coral necklace because it was a family possession until our mother donated it for a church bazaar. That card was the one she included with her gift. It was the usual thing to do in those days, so that notes of thanks could be written to all donors."

"Given away as a prize?" said Teresa, losing all hope of finding out anything else about it. She was about to wrap the box up when Selina took it out of her hand.

"It's been a long time," she said, almost caressing the small box. "Remember the man who won it, Gloria? How very excited he was that night."

"What was his name?" asked Teresa quickly. "Do you remember it?"

"Remember it, we have never forgotten it, and often wonder what has become of him. You see, a bazaar draws visitors from all parts of town and nearby villages. They come and go. This man was a rare visitor and a talker, besides."

Teresa thought she would never come to the point and answer her question. Selina was having a good time reminiscing while she and Mercedes hung onto her words, waiting.

"Before he left the booth," Selina continued, "he told our mother he and his wife had been brought up in El Refugio, the orphanage for children. They had left it when they became of age, and had met years later in Guayama, where they got married."

"You have not told us his name," said Mercedes.

"Ah, yes, his name. Julián Ramón Santiago, that was it, and his wife was Amalia. He kept mentioning her all the time and saying that the coral necklace would make a grand gift for her."

"Julián Ramón Santiago," said Teresa, certain now that he must have been Ramón's father.

Selina looked at the creased card in the box. "Mother would have never guessed when she put this card in the box that it would come to play such a decisive part in the life of that young man's son!" She replaced the card and gave the box back to Teresa.

The door opened and a group of little children ran into the room chanting their greetings. *"Buenas tardes, Señorita* Selina y *Señorita* Gloria."

*"Buenas tardes, niños,"* said Selina, turning her attention to them.

"These are our nursery, school children," explained Gloria. "Mother always had a nursery school for children in the neighborhood, and we have continued with it."

Teresa nodded as she tried to wrap the sandalwood box in the handkerchief again, before Selina had a chance to come back. *"Cielos!"* Teresa said to herself, "how she can talk!" She thanked Gloria and promised she would bring Ramón to the house next time they were in town.

Teresa opened the door quietly while Selina was busy explaining to the children about the two-tone color of the alphabet on the blackboard. Followed by Mercedes, she tiptoed outside.

As they stood there, the church bell struck twelve.

"Noon, Teresa," said Mercedes, starting to run. "Sixta will be leaving without us if we don't hurry."

When the two arrived at Martín's place, Sixta was sitting on a long bench waiting. Their two horses stood at the door where Martín had left them before going to lunch himself.

The girls slumped down beside Sixta and tried to catch their breaths.

"You look as if you have been chased all over town. Where were you?" asked Sixta.

"At 26 Tamarindo," said Mercedes.

"Why, that's the Ayalas' house. What were you doing so far uptown?"

"Finding out about Ramón's family, and now we know it all," explained Teresa.

Sixta looked from one girl to the other, not quite able to get the real meaning of what they were saying. Finally Teresa began from the beginning and gave her a complete account. When she finished, Sixta was as excited as they were.

"Let's not stop on the road for lunch," she said. "I want to ride straight to the *finca* with you. Ramón must hear this news as soon as possible.

They way back seemed longer only because they wanted to get there in such a hurry. Sixta led the way and Teresa managed with difficulty to keep up with her. At last they came within view of the house. They climbed up the hill and rode to the rear, coming to a stop near the woodshed. They could hear the family's voices coming from the open shed.

"Ramón! Ramón!" called Teresa.

He ran to help them dismount and lead the horses away.

"Tie them here," said Teresa, "and come with us to the shed. We have news for you." She picked up the lunch basket and ran ahead to meet the family.

"Oh, *Mamá*," she said, laying the lunch basket on the ground.

"We have heard all about Ramón's parents."

"About Ramon's parents? Really, Teresa?" said her mother. "Where could you have heard about them when your father has tried all these years without success?"

"But we did, at 26 Tamarindo."

Ramón had come back and stood waiting to hear what Teresa had to say, his face glowing with excitement.

Teresa opened the lunch basket and took the sandalwood box out. "I never knew there was a card here until Mercedes took out the necklace to try it on. Right at this address we found two women who had known your father, Ramón. This necklace was your mother's." She passed the card to him to see.

"What else did the women say?" asked Ramón.

"One of them told us how your father had won the necklace at a church bazaar and had given it to your mother as a gift."

"And how they had been brought up in El Refugio," said Mercedes, "until they grew up and got married."

The two girls took turns telling the story as they had heard it from Selina.

As their story continued, all eyes were on Ramón, on whose face was an expression of joy as they had never seen before.

To any other group not acquainted with Ramón's story, what the girls had said might have sounded fantastic, but for the Rodrigo family, who for years had struggled to get a clue that might have thrown more light on his past, the reality of the things they now heard was the fulfillment of a long search come suddenly to an end.

"Ramón Santiago," said Don Rodrigo, calling him by his full name. His arms were soon around him as he kept repeating his name over and over.

Doña Anita watched the two with blurred eyes. She knew what the news had meant to her husband, for he was seldom carried away by emotion.

But it was Ramón who was the happiest of them all.

"Let us blow the conch shell," he said, "and let every worker at the *finca* hear the news."

"Yes, yes," said Teresa, running into the house to get it.

When she came back, they gathered at the edge of the hill, and Ramón blew a long, sharp note.

Out in the fields the workers heard it and stopped their work.

"It's Don Rodrigo's call," said Felipe. "Let us go."

One by one, they followed him eagerly, wondering what the summons might mean. At the top of the hill, Ramón waited to share with them the most important news he had ever had.

# CHAPTER 11
# RAMÓN SANTIAGO

Ramón pulled himself up straight and stretched out his arms to ease his tired back. He had been working all morning tilling a patch of land for planting. The sun beat mercilessly on his head, and the perspiration which matted his hair ran down his face. It might have been Sunday, for the serenity and quietness which surrounded him. Yet far away across the hill, he knew the peasants were busy working too, getting ready the new tobacco sheds Don Rodrigo had ordered built.

"Ramón Santiago," he said softly at first, and then louder. He listened to the sound of his voice. He was beginning to get used to the new addition to his name. No more doubts, no more hours of wishful thinking and the secret hope every time a letter arrived at the *finca*. Nothing now but satisfaction and peace of mind. "Ramón Santiago," he said again as he dried the perspiration on his face. Soon, he would have time to leave the *finca* and visit Guayama to pick up the trail of his parents. Then, finally, many more questions would be answered to his satisfaction.

A week had gone by since Doña Anita suggested that Teresa share the coral necklace with Mercedes. He was glad that now the two girls, to whom he owed his status of mind, shared his mother's only treasure.

"Ramón Santiago!" called someone across the field.

"Ho!" he answered.

It was Esteban, carrying a sack on his back, followed by Antonio skipping along behind.

"I went to Vázquez's *finca* with Esteban," said Antonio, stretching out under a tree.

Esteban threw his sack on the ground and sat next to him.

"What's in the sack?" asked Ramón.

"Potatoes for seeding," he answered. "Bought them this morning."

"I am going to help plant them," said Antonio.

"He is a great help to me, Ramón. How is it that you don't get him to give you a hand."

Ramón laughed.

"The further he can get from the house, the happier he is. When he is not tramping behind Mercedes and Teresa, he is at your house. Do you know why, though?"

Esteban shook his head.

"Afraid of the *cartilla*. You should see the face he puts on for everyone to see when his mother makes him sit all day next to Grandmother with his *cartilla* in his hands."

"I thought you said you liked to read the lessons of the *cartilla*," said Esteban.

"Only when Teresa is away at school and Manolo has gone back to his aunt in Cayey," said Ramón.

Antonio kept his thoughts to himself. He knew Ramón was right. He could always go back to the *cartilla* after the summer, when there was no one in the house but Grandmother and Doña Anita. But when Teresa came back and Manolo returned, he had little time then for it.

"The fact is," said Esteban, as he listened to Ramón, "that Antonio is acting in exactly the same way you did when you were his age. Remember how you used to follow me about the place? And how Don Rodrigo always answered my special call for you by appearing at the door with his cigar in his mouth? Long before he had time to shake the ashes off, I had started running downhill."

Antonio began to laugh. The idea of Esteban running away from Don Rodrigo seemed ridiculous to him.

"I don't think you cared much for the *cartilla*," said Esteban.

"You had to read the *cartilla*, too?" asked Antonio.

"Read it? Wait until Grandmother starts drilling her *cuatro ramas*."

"What's that?"

"Addition, subtraction, multiplication and division, four branches which she says lead up to the tree of knowledge."

"Will I have to learn them, too?"

"You ask Teresa," said Ramón.

The sound of the conch shell came over the hill.

"Lunch," said Antonio, jumping up and starting to run towards the house.

"That's the only sound that brings him home from wherever he may be," said Ramón, watching him go.

"I guess I better go, too."

Esteban picked up his sack of potatoes, and the two walked as far as the foot of the hill. "*Adiós*, Ramón Santiago," he said. "I hope Lucía has a good lunch."

Ramón waved back as he ran up the hill. When he reached the house, he found Grandmother showing the girls how to transfer the piece of lace they had finished to the beginning of the pattern.

"Come and see," called Teresa, "we have a whole pattern done, and it looks as good as Grandmother's."

"Almost," he corrected her.

"Almost?" said Mercedes. "What do you think, Grandmother? Isn't it just as good as yours?"

"Just as good as the very first I made," she answered. "But by next summer, no one will be able to tell the difference, not me."

When they went in for lunch, the mail was on the table. Mercedes went through it quickly, looking for a letter from her father. "Why doesn't he write?" she said, putting the letters down again.

"He does not trust himself with the surprise," Don Rodrigo said. "A letter might give him away."

"I wonder what it will be?" said Mercedes, helping herself to a platter of fried ripe plantains Lucía had set near her.

"Remember what Sixta said, Mercedes. Wait without too much planning, then the surprise will be a real one." Teresa imitated Sixta's voice.

"You only quote her in fun," said Mercedes. "Since we found the Ayala family, you have lost interest in the surprise. Not even Ramón talks about it anymore. I alone care now."

"We all care," said Doña Anita. "Do you think Lucio would have written Rodrigo if he had meant the surprise just for you?"

"I agree with Sixta," Grandmother ventured to say. "Regardless of your feelings, Mercedes, the surprise will lose its interest to all of us if we do nothing but wonder all day about it."

"I do think more about it than I like to talk," said Teresa. "I am doing what Sixta suggested.

There are all kinds of surprises to bring home when one has gone all over the island practically."

Lucía came to clear the table.

"I have brought up the case of glass jars, Grandmother," she said.

"Good," said Grandmother. "The girls can start washing them now. Is that Antonio I heard about the kitchen? Have him help with the drying. Unless this work is finished today, there won't be guava picking tomorrow."

There were other chores around the house the girls would much rather do, but when they remembered the picnic that went with picking guavas, washing dusty glasses did not seem to matter at all. They followed Lucía to the kitchen, where she prepared two basins for them: one with broken pieces of soap and another with clear water.

Teresa washed, Mercedes rinsed and Antonio dried.

Ramón stayed away from the fields and gave the girls a hand. He carried the glass jars to the table near the charcoal stove, where they would be within Grandmother's reach. Then he rinsed the large pieces of cheesecloth used to pass the guava pulp through, and hung them to dry. When he finished, he measured the sugar and set it on Grandmother's table. He even brought in the large kettles where the guavas were to be boiled, and scrubbed them clean. Everything was ready now. Nothing was missing but the guavas, and those they would bring tomorrow after they had their picnic.

"Let's go and ask Sixta to come along with us," said Teresa.

"I doubt if she'll go," said Grandmother. "I hear she has a new order of handkerchieves from Cidra, larger than she has ever had from any other place. But try, a day away from work will do her good."

"Come, let us try anyhow, Mercedes," said Teresa, racing out of the house.

"Ramón Santiago!" It was Don Rodrigo calling from the other side of the house.

Ramón smiled at the sound of his complete name and went to his call.

# CHAPTER 12
# HURRICANE!

The next day, Doña Anita was up at six o'clock, ready to fix the lunch basket. It was unusually hot for so early in the morning, and she opened the kitchen door and stopped it with a large stone to let more air in.

Lucía had left pieces of chicken she fried for the children wrapped in wax paper on the table. Next to it were two boxes of crackers and a jar of chopped ham.

Doña Anita began to make the sandwiches, adding chopped green peppers to the ham, the way Teresa liked them. Cheese, bananas and oranges went into the basket, along with some sweet-potato candy left over from dessert. After the basket was fixed, she folded a towel over it and put the basket on the table. Beads of perspiration covered her brow. She had been working faster than she had realized. She heard footsteps in the dining room. It was Grandmother.

"Why, Anita, you got here before I did. Why didn't you let me do the sandwiches?"

"I wish I had. It is so hot, my head is aching. I wonder if we ought to let the girls go out. There's bound to be rain sooner or later."

They looked out of the door at the faraway hills.

"Nonsense," said Grandmother, "this is regular August weather. Let the girls take the large straw hats and come back as soon as they eat their lunch."

"There's Antonio and Lucía coming up the hill. What do you suppose is keeping the girls, *Mamá*?"

"Nothing is keeping us. Here we are," said Teresa as she came into the kitchen followed by Mercedes and Ramón. "I don't want any breakfast, *Mamá*. Why can't we leave right now?"

"*Buenos días*," said Lucía and Antonio.

"What is that you are carrying, Antonio?" asked Mercedes, looking at the bundle under his arm.

"It's a sack," he said. "I want to fill it with guavas."

"And who is going to help you carry it? Mercedes will have to help me with the basket," said Teresa, "and you are supposed to help Ramón with his."

"I can bring the basket alone," said Ramón, lifting the lunch basket to try it's weight. We'll see if Antonio can bring his sack alone, too."

While they ate their breakfast, Grandmother stood at the door mopping her forehead. "How about waiting until tomorrow for the guavas?" she said. "There is rain in the air."

"No, please, Grandmother," pleaded Teresa. "If it rains, it will only be a summer shower."

"All right, then go and get the straw hats, and come back as soon as possible from the grove," said Grandmother.

Ramón picked up the lunch basket and Antonio his sack, and they followed after the girls.

"Keep away from the wire fences, Antonio," called his mother. "Last year you left part of your trousers along with some of your skin as well."

The guava grove was on the other side of the cow path. Don Rodrigo had circled it with rows and rows of barbed wire to keep the cows away. It was the only guava grove at the *finca*, but it yielded a large crop.

The children had not walked very far when they began to feel the heat. The girls took off their hats and fanned their faces.

"I'm thirsty," said Antonio.

"Give him an orange," said Teresa. "We can sit here while he eats it."

"He can have the orange," said Ramón, "but we won't sit. If we do, we'll never get to the grove until late at the rate you're walking."

On the way downhill, they met Benito and Valentín.

"Better take it easy," they said. "It's almost too hot to be picking guavas, and it looks like a storm is coming."

When they finally reached the grove, Ramón looked for a shady place and began to empty the lunch basket.

No amount of heat ever lessened Antonio's appetite, and he sat down ready to eat his share.

"Come, Antonio," said Teresa. "We must first pick the guavas."

Reluctantly, he picked up his sack and followed her to where the bushes were lowest.

Teresa and Mercedes placed their basket between them and began to work. Ramón chose the higher trees where the guavas were larger.

"How is your sack coming along, Antonio?" he called after a while.

He turned around expecting to find him working close to the girls, but Antonio was not there.

"Where did he go, Teresa?"

"I don't know, he was here a minute ago. Antonio!" she called.

"Antonio!" called Ramón, but no one answered.

They went back to where the lunch was left. Maybe he had decided to eat, after all. Maybe the heat was too much for him, and he had decided to go home. But Antonio was not there either.

"It's no use," said Ramón. "Stay here, and I'll go around the grove. He must be somewhere near."

He looked behind some of the bushes for fear Antonio might be staging one of his hide and seek games. Only ripe guavas dropped from the bushes as he brushed against them. Ramón came close to one of the wire fences, and something moved in the thick underbrush. What could it be? The grove was wired so close that no cow could get through, and he knew there weren't any wild animals or snakes at the *finca*. Probably birds, he thought, noticing the amount of pecked guavas on the ground. Just then the branches shook briskly and a shower of fruit came tumbling down.

"There," said a voice, "now I have enough."

"Antonio," called Ramón, recognizing his voice. He parted the branches and looked in. Stretched on the ground comfortably filling his sack was Antonio.

"Antonio," called Ramón, recognizing his voice. He parted the branches and looked in. Stretched on the ground comfortably filling his sack was Antonio.

"Look, Ramón," he cried joyfully, "my sack is full already." He crawled out pulling the sack behind him.

"I have seen enough," Ramón said. "Come along now."

When they joined the girls, Antonio was in high spirits.

"I have finished," he said. "Now I can eat."

"Eat, eat," said Teresa. "Is there anything else you ever think of?" She fanned her face and dried her forehead. The heat seemed to be rising by the minute.

"We were worried about you," said Mercedes. "Why did you go away?"

"Worried? Why?"

"Never mind," said Ramón, trying to compromise. "Come and help me fill my basket. We'll work near each other where the branches are low."

They all resumed their work and for a while nothing but the muffled sound of the guavas falling into the baskets was heard.

Ramón's shirt was so wet that it stuck to his body.

"Let's not pick any more," he said. "It's much too hot."

They left their baskets under the branches and went back to where the lunch was. Mercedes and Teresa stretched out on the grass, but the heat coming from the earth made them jump to their feet again.

"Open the sandwiches, Mercedes," said Ramón, stretching the towel on the grass as a tablecloth.

Teresa opened the boxes of crackers and began to cut slices of cheese to put on them.

By the time the lunch was spread out, a rare yellow hue had come over the field, as if a colored glass had been suddenly put before the sun. A sharp gust of wind sent the paper wrappers high into the air.

Ramón remembered Grandmother's warning. It was going to rain after all.

Another gust of wind blew over them with such force that it staggered Antonio.

"We better go," said Ramón.

"Go?" said Antonio. "I thought we were going to eat."

Ramón ran to where his basket was, emptied the fruit and brought it back. "Help me put the food back in," he told the girls. "We will eat at home."

He had scarcely finished his remark when three sharp blasts sounded in the air. Ramón stood still, fear written all over his face.

It was the sign that a hurricane had been announced.

Teresa reached for Mercedes, and they both started to run across the fields towards home.

Ramón reached for Antonio, but he wriggled out of his hand and ran back to the place where he had left his sack.

"My guavas, I want my guavas," he cried.

Ramón, certain that Antonio did not know what the blasts meant, ran after him as he bent to pick up the sack of guavas. Ramón pulled him away, but Antonio would not let go, so he snatched the sack out of his hands, flung it over his shoulders and ran across the fields, dragging Antonio along.

When they reached home the rain had started to fall. Don Rodrigo stood still, clutching the conch.

He was at the center of the family group, listening to the peasant who had brought the news from town about the approaching hurricane. According to his report, the hurricane was not due to strike for two more hours, provided it did not alter its course or blow out to sea.

"Hurry to your rooms," said Grandmother to Mercedes and Teresa, who stood like stone figures by her side. "Put some of your clothes in your trunks, then hurry back to the front room."

Once in their rooms, both girls worked like robots, scarcely conscious of what they were throwing into their trunks. Teresa finished first and then went to get her friend. When she opened her door, Teresa found Mercedes sitting on top of her trunk crying. Many of the clothes she had intended to put away were scattered all over the floor.

"Don't cry," said Teresa, beginning to pick up the things. "This is a strong house, and nothing will happen." She wanted to believe that, too, and she was not sure Mercedes did.

"A hurricane, Teresa, and I don't even know where *Papá* is. At least we are all here together, but *Papá* . . . who knows where he really is?" She began to cry again, and Teresa found it difficult to comfort her. She would be doing the same if she were away from her parents at a time like this.

"Let's go back to the front room, Mercedes," she finally said. "Grandmother must be waiting for us."

They made their way through piles of furniture and heavy barrels filled with dishes. Lucía, Grandmother and Doña Anita were busy storing staples into a basket, which they covered with oilcloth. The noise within the house rose so that they could not hear each other's voices. Boards were nailed inside as well as outside on doors and windows, and bureau drawers were barricaded against the wall. Three large trunks were set together and placed in the dining room for the family to sit on. When the nailing and hammering subsided, the sound of the rain on the roof and the whistling of the wind through the trees seemed to have acquired immense proportions.

"Lock the kitchen door, Ramón," shouted Don Rodrigo as he rolled two barrels against the front-room door.

Teresa and her parents sat on one trunk, Ramón, Mercedes and Grandmother on the other, and Lucia with Antonio buried in her lap sat on the one at the end.

It was a strange thing to sit and wait when you knew that a hurricane was coming along. They huddled together, listening to the outside world, which already was being torn apart.

Suddenly a roaring sound, like a million human voices hissing and howling at once, filled the house.

"The wind! Mother of God, save us," said Doña Anita.

"*Papá, Papá,*" cried Mercedes, starting to sob again.

With a loud crash, a sheet of corrugated zinc struck the kitchen door, rending it in two. Water seeped through, slowly at first, then freely until it covered the entire floor.

"Stand on the trunks," cried Don Rodrigo as Ramón dashed towards the door, trying to reinforce the hinges, which were already loose. With difficulty, he tried to nail an extra board across it. The damaged door creaked and shook, as if it were being pushed from outside by a superhuman force.

"Look out," shouted Don Rodrigo, holding the board that Ramón was nailing. But it was too late. The force of the wind had severed the rest of the door, and the whirlwind that filled the empty space caught Ramón and dragged him outside.

"Ramón, Ramón," he called, letting the board go and dashing after him.

A scream came from the place where the family stood. Outside, plants and uprooted trees lay everywhere. The shed where the Feast of the Cross had been held was no longer there.

Don Rodrigo swayed back and forth trying with difficulty to stay on his feet. "Ramón!" he called again and again. Only the sound of the wind came back in answer. He leaned against the end of the house and looked around. It was then that he saw

Ramón, caught among the branches of a large tree which had fallen against the stable door.

Groping his way, half-crouched to avoid the wind, he made his way to Ramón.

Ramón lay on his side holding to the trunk of the tree. There was a cut on his forehead. Don Rodrigo helped him to his feet and, with his arms around his shoulders, managed to get back to the house where the family nervously waited.

"Make room for him on the trunks," said Don Rodrigo, but Ramón refused to lay down.

Grandmother examined his cut and was relieved to see that it was only skin-deep. She tore up a towel and began to wash the gash, while Lucía kept pouring water from an earthen jug. With the rest of the towel, she improvised a bandage and tied his head. Then she opened one of the trunks and took out an old wool blanket and wrapped it around his shoulders.

Teresa, Mercedes and Antonio stood watching, seemingly not yet able to realize that he was safe. When they had heard Don Rodrigo calling Ramón, they had come back to the kitchen only to find it empty. Their personal fears were gone, only anxiety for Ramón filled their hearts. Nothing else seemed to matter.

So engrossed was the rest of the family in ministering help to Ramón that they did not notice that suddenly the rain had stopped and the wind had ceased. Could it actually be true? They were not sure. They knew that lulls sometimes meant that the hurricane would return, tearing and destroying worse than before. So they waited. For minutes they sat close to each other. It seemed like hours, but it was no lull. The hurricane was really gone.

# CHAPTER 13
# AFTERMATH

The next morning, the children awoke to find the sun shining and the sky so blue and clear that the experiences of the day before seemed to have been a nightmare. Only when they looked outside their windows, the devastation that met their eyes brought the reality of those few hours back to them.

They were surprised to see Ramón up and ready to follow Don Rodrigo on his inspection trip about the *finca*. A small wad of cotton held by a piece of adhesive tape had replaced the makeshift bandage on his head. Like Don Rodrigo, he had heavy boots on and he carried a machete to clear out paths obstructed by fallen trees and branches.

Felipe came up the hill with a group of peasants and began to give a grim picture of what he had seen on his way.

"All the tobacco sheds are down, Don Rodrigo," he said. "Whatever escaped the velocity of the wind has been washed off by the rain. Even the patches of coffee under the trees beyond Gregorio's house are gone, swept away as if they had never been there. Two peasants from Vázquez's *finca* were struck down by trees and killed.

The girls looked quickly at Ramón and thanked God he had been spared. Don Rodrigo listened solemnly as Felipe went on and on with his tale of woe.

"What is there to do?" asked the workers who had stood almost humbly looking at Don Rodrigo with their brown eyes full of despair.

"Yes," said Felipe, "what is there to do?"

"Work," Don Rodrigo answered. "Work until every house is repaired and the land is cleared, then plant again. There is no other alternative."

He turned to his wife. "Open the stockroom, Anita," he said. "No worker on my *finca* shall go wanting while there is food at home. Now let us go; there is much to be done before the sun goes down."

If for a minute Don Rodrigo had underestimated Felipe's words, the sight that met his eyes as he tramped over debris and mud left no doubt of the plight the entire island must have been in. He earnestly hoped the hurricane had struck with less force on some other parts. He would have to get to town at the first chance he had and see what the news was there before he could make any other plans.

They passed Sixta's house and saw her brother resetting the windows the wind had severed. His vegetable garden was down.

"I would go with you," he called after them, "if I had not this work to do before night descends upon us."

Sixta and her mother came out of the house to inquire about the family, and Don Rodrigo told them about the stockroom being open. They too could call if they needed food.

Further down, the road was tangled by fallen trees and they had to cut their way through to reach the shortcut to the *finca*.

As they approached the big tamarind tree, they could hear the sound of nailing and hammering coming from the peasants' quarters. The old tree stood erect, its branches bare of leaves, while all about its trunk laid a mass of twisted young trees, as if in their final struggle with the wind they had reached to it for help.

When the peasants saw Don Rodrigo, they began to wail, pointing to the destruction outside and inside their houses.

Their children surrounded Don Rodrigo wide-eyed and still frightened.

"The hurricane is past," said Don Rodrigo, trying to sound casual. "What is lost won't come back to us. We must be thankful there were no deaths on our *finca*."

Before he left, he told them that Doña Anita had opened the stockroom. Those who needed food could call. He looked at the children. "Antonio, Teresa and Mercedes are all working at home," he said to them. "You, too, can help here also. By using the shortcut you can bring the groceries home to your mothers."

Benito said the spring was swollen, and the peasants were using three large trees which had fallen across it as bridges to get across.

"That means the river is impassable, too," Don Rodrigo said. "Let's go back to the road. I want to see how clean it really is."

Meanwhile up at the house, Doña Anita sat in front of the small window in the stockroom, greeting the *peons* who came along to get their share of groceries. Men, women and children came, and none left without giving their version of their experiences. By the time the last one had come and gone, Doña Anita and the girls had a clear picture of conditions about the *finca*. It was with relief that they finally closed the window, pulled out empty boxes and sat to rest.

Teresa and Mercedes felt as if their arms weren't part of their bodies. Neither of the girls had ever worked so fast or hard before in the stockroom. Even Antonio, who had been running back and forth delivering the packages, was too tired to even talk.

He crouched on the floor next to them and also tried to rest.

The experiences of the day before came back to them. It was their first hurricane, one they would find hard to forget.

"Teresa!" Grandmother's voice rang through the hall, calling.

Mercedes and Antonio followed Teresa out of the room.

A heavy scent filled the hall. Teresa sniffed.

"Guavas, overripe guavas," she said.

Grandmother was standing in the center of the neck, holding a sack.

"My guavas," shouted Antonio. "Where were they, Grandmother?"

"Behind Rodrigo's desk," she answered. "How did they ever get there?"

"I don't know," he said. "All I know is that those are the guavas I picked."

No one had noticed as Ramón and Don Rodrigo came into the neck until they were standing close by.

"So here is where I dropped them?" said Ramón. "I was so busy pushing furniture, nailing windows and doors, and running back and forth from the barn that I really didn't remember where I had left the sack of guavas."

"Those are priceless guavas," said Don Rodrigo. "They are the only ones left at the *finca*, and the last we will see for a long time."

"You can make jelly, Grandmother," said Teresa.

"We shall make it," Grandmother said. "Each of you shall have a glass, but none will be larger than Antonio's who saved the last guavas of the *finca*."

Antonio was so pleased that he carried the sack to the kitchen to tell his mother the news.

After dinner, the family gathered to hear Don Rodrigo tell about his scouting trip in and about the *finca*. Then, still worried by the affairs of the day, they retired to their rooms, where their tired bodies tried to rest.

Long after they had left, Don Rodrigo sat in front of his desk, apparently reading from a book which lay open before him. But his eyes were not following the printed page. They were closed, his mind brimming with ideas and plans which came clearly now and set the pattern for the course he was to follow. There was no alternative. He took out the map of the *finca* and studied it, concentrating on the area which represented his tobacco plots. He had seen them today sodded with water, almost ruined. When would they flourish again with the rich tobacco leaves they were so famous for? He had ordered Felipe to get more workers and begin building new sheds.

He would prepare again. When the time was ripe for planting, nothing would keep him from a new start. The more he consulted the map, the surer he was of his new plans. He would tell the family just as soon as he had time to visit Cidra and Cayey. Summer was almost gone, and school would soon be open. Where in the world could Lucio be, wondered Don Rodrigo? They had not heard from him even after the hurricane.

Don Rodrigo folded the map and put it away, then blew the lamp out and stood in the darkness looking out the open window. The sky was brilliant with stars. It seemed to him that all their twinkle somehow could not compare with the glow that came from his fireflies. It was dark outside, and for once there were no magic lights at the *finca*.

He closed the window and, feeling along the wall, found his way to his room.

# CHAPTER 14
# LUCIO'S SURPRISE

There was laughter and talk in the kitchen once more, for Grandmother was making her guava jelly.

The girls hovered about her, watching the preparations and offering their help whenever they could. But it was really Grandmother and Lucía, masters at such an art, who had things in hand. The girls' help had been relegated to filling the glass jars after the jelly was made.

Antonio sat outside the kitchen door, waiting patiently for the time when he would collect his special gift. As he sat there, the sound of a horse trotting below reached his ears. He ran to the edge of the hill to see who the horseman could be. He did not recognize him, but there was no doubt that the rider was headed for the house. He ran back to the kitchen with the news.

"There's a horseman coming up the hill, come and see."

The girls followed him.

The horseman was almost up now, and Mercedes let out a cry that brought the rest of the family out of the house, for the rider was her father.

"*Papá, Papá!*" she shouted, jumping about his horse as if she were skipping over a bed of hot coals.

"Well, Lucio," said Don Rodrigo, "you have found your way back home at last. Where in the world have you been?"

"Everywhere, Rodrigo, including the island of Vieques."

They went into the house.

"Where did the hurricane catch up with you?" Grandmother asked.

"In Las Mareas, worse place to be caught. A hurricane on the seacoast always seems worse than in the interior. But look at the girls' faces. There is only one thing on their minds: my surprise. Well, here it is. We are going to be neighbors, Rodrigo."

"What do you mean?" asked Don Rodrigo.

"I have bought Vázquez's *finca*."

"Bought Vázquez's *finca*?" echoed the family.

"How did you do it, Lucio? I have been after that land for years," said Don Rodrigo.

"Through a close friend of his. Vázquez wanted to sell to an outsider. Why, I don't know, nor do I care."

"So the miser is leaving the land," said Don Rodrigo with certain relief. "I can't say that I regret it. If the land was to go to someone, I'm glad it went to you."

Teresa, Mercedes and Antonio were all ready to start towards the *finca* at once, had they not been stopped by Doña Anita.

"What a surprise," said Ramón, glad to know that their closest neighbor was to be Lucio.

"Aren't you glad you came to the *finca* beforehand, Mercedes?" said Teresa. "Now you know all about it."

"Too bad this hurricane had to come along," said Grandmother. "All the *fincas* have been badly hit around these parts."

"I would have bought the land even after the hurricane," Lucio said. "The proximity to Rodrigo's *finca* was the thing that really mattered to me."

"They say Vázquez has money buried on his land," said Ramón. "I can see Mercedes and Teresa digging for treasure next summer."

Lucio laughed. "Of all the eccentricities I have heard about the man, that is one I don't believe, although I am sure Mercedes won't agree with me."

Next, Lucio turned to a more important subject. "How about workers, Rodrigo? I shall be in need of some, especially one person well acquainted with the land, one I can leave in charge until next summer when I move in. Someone like your Felipe or Ramón. By the way, why not let me have Ramón for the time being?"

Don Rodrigo shook his head. "I have other plans for him, plans which I have not yet told the family, Lucio. Since we are on the subject, I see no reason to keep them a secret any longer. I have decided to take the family to San Juan for the rest of the year, and leave Ramón here in charge."

Ramón's eyes sparkled with joy. In charge of the *finca*! He had never thought that really could happen. The family, too, was taken by surprise. When had Rodrigo come to such a conclusion? But a year away from the *finca*, especially during such times, would be the best thing after all.

Lucio was disappointed at having lost Ramón's help.

"Is there anyone else on your *finca* you can spare?" he asked.

"No, but there is Esteban, although he is not part of the *finca*. Like Ramón, he has grown up around here and has managed his small place well. He has done work for Vázquez, and is liked by the peasants."

"The boy is dependable," said Doña Anita. "You remember, Sixta, the young woman you met here the day you came? Esteban is her brother, two years older than she is. He is a born farmer."

"There's Sixta now," said Grandmother.

The girls met her at the door. Sixta had brought the new dresses.

"Put them on," she whispered, "and let me see how you look in them."

The girls rushed to their rooms.

When they came back again, not only did they have on the new dresses, but their coral necklaces and earrings as well. Teresa looked much taller in her new princess dress, while the sash on Mercedes yellow organdy made her look like a little girl dressed up in her Sunday clothes.

Lucio asked where Mercedes had found the jewelry. He knew he had not seen it before.

"They turned detectives one day," said Don Rodrigo. "That is the prize she received for the part she played in straightening things out."

While the girls stood showing their dresses, Don Rodrigo told Lucio the rest of the story.

Grandmother had not seen such fine work as Sixta had turned out on the dresses.

"Your place is in town, Sixta, and not at a *finca*," she said. "You can have a place of your own and a good clientele."

"But I don't want a place of my own, Grandmother. I would not trade a schoolroom full of children for the biggest shop in San Juan."

"Sixta only wants to teach," said Teresa. "So do we."

"You have a long time to wait," said her mother. "Go and take off your new dresses. You will have plenty of time to wear them in San Juan."

Doña Anita turned to Sixta. "They are beautiful," she said. "I could not have done half as well. Why don't you consider *Mamá's* suggestion? There is a quality in your work that is very different from any other sewing I have seen. It comes out even in your lace orders. That is a thing worth preserving."

Sixta listened to Doña Anita expound her theories, but she was sure all of Doña Anita's talking could not dissuade her from her original plans. Not when there were children at *fincas* who could not read or write. She would teach. Let those who wanted to sew spend their time doing that.

Don Rodrigo interrupted the trend of conversation to ask Sixta if her brother was home. When she told him that he was, the three men left, followed by Antonio, who was anxious to hear what Esteban would answer to Lucio's proposition.

When they were gone, Doña Anita told Sixta about Lucio's plans for her brother.

"Oh, Doña Anita, I never thought Lucio's surprise would include us, too. Heaven only knows what it means to our family. I must hurry home. I want to thank him myself."

"Not before I pay for the dresses," said Doña Anita.

"Pay for the dresses? This is a present for the girls, Doña Anita. You do not owe me anything."

Grandmother insisted that she accept her pay, especially after the hurricane. Even Teresa and

Mercedes pleaded with her, but Sixta held her ground. Two hurricanes could not have made her change her mind. The work on the dresses was meant as a present, and she wanted them to accept them as such.

There was nothing else to do but thank her, and Sixta left. Downhill with a light foot and still lighter heart, she hurried to her home. Esteban's good fortune was the beginning of a turn for the best in her life. No more would she have to sit summer after summer turning out work like a machine after studying hard all year at the university. Maybe next summer, she, too, could enjoy the *finca* as much as she did when she was a child.

When Sixta reached home, the house was empty except for her mother, who was singing in the kitchen. Sixta knew her brother had accepted his new job; her mother's song was one of thanksgiving.

# CHAPTER 15
# *ADIÓS*—FAREWELL

Lucio left for San Juan soon after things were straightened out with Esteban. Since his departure, life at the *finca* went on at a great pace.

Doña Anita and Grandmother packed things they were to take away, as well as things which were to be left behind.

Teresa and Mercedes cut off the rest of their bobbin-pin lace and stored the bobbin pins and patterns away in boxes ready to be used the following summer. They packed their trunks and stored sachets of dry patchouli between their clothes.

When they finished, they spent days walking about the *finca*, saying goodbye to the workers. Pilar invited the girls to spend the afternoon with her, and later she and Felipe took the girls through some of Lucio's new *finca*.

Teresa asked Felipe to say goodbye to Martín for them the next time he went to Cayey, and Mercedes sent word to come and visit her *finca* next summer, when she would be living there.

The girls saw less of Ramón now, for he was always away. When he came to the house, he spent hours talking with Don Rodrigo, discussing the projects about the *finca*, making sure all things were clear to him before he left.

Don Rodrigo had not been able to hire a large coach in Cayey or Cidra for the family, so he had written Lucio to contact Filimón and arrange things accordingly. He had been waiting for his answer. In the meantime, he was busy seeing to the number of peasants who daily came looking for work. Some of the ones he hired he sent to Felipe, while others he sent along to Esteban.

At last one morning, among the letters a peasant brought from Cayey, was the letter from Lucio. It was full of good news. He had contacted Filimón, who would come to the *finca* Wednesday morning. He had also found an empty house on the corner of Cristo and San Francisco Streets. It had eight rooms with a balcony in the front and a gallery on the back. It was a two-story, and he was sure that on Sundays they could even hear the concerts played by the Municipal Band on the Baldorioty Plaza.

"Wednesday is only day after tomorrow," said Doña Anita. "We did well to get things ready ahead of time."

Word spread about that the date for leaving had been set, and the peasants began to call to say goodbye to the family.

Wednesday turned out warm and humid. Early in the morning the packages and trunks were brought to the front room, and after breakfast the family sat to wait for the coach. Grandmother sat with Filo on her lap, stroking the cat's soft fur. Filo was going along to San Juan, too, and she purred contently as if she approved of Grandmother's plan.

Outside in the rear of the house, Ramón sat on a bench carving. Close at hand was a coconut cup he had finished. It had a letter T in the center and a fine border of ferns at the top. Chips flew from the quick whittling of his knife. He was putting the finishing touches on a letter M in the center of another cup. Tiny fireflies formed a fringe around the cup. A smile came to his face as he remembered Mercedes' excitement when she had first seen the fireflies at the *finca*.

He smoothed his work with a piece of sandpaper, glad he had finished it before the family left. As he stood admiring his work, Teresa and Mercedes came around the house, looking for him. He tried to hide the cups, but the girls had seen them and knew by his action that the cups were meant for them.

"Let us see them," said Mercedes.

"I was bringing them to the coach," he said. "Now that you are here, you might as well have them beforehand."

"How beautiful they are, Ramón!" said Teresa, admiring hers.

"We can actually use them to drink our coffee," said Mercedes.

There was a sound of wheels on the road, and the three ran to the front of the house in time to see Filimón's coach stop at the gate.

"It's the coach, *Papá*," cried Teresa.

Filimón came up the path, holding his straw hat high in greeting to the family.

"Don Rodrigo," he said, "my coach in its full 'vestiment' awaits." There was a certain flourish in his remark that expressed his pleasure.

The coach was gaily decorated with a border of red fringe on the top, and the sides were bright and shiny. It was evident Filimón had worked hard to show his special coach at its very best.

"Where is Antonio?" asked Teresa, looking at the crowd of peasants who had come to see the family leave.

Ramón shrugged his shoulders. "Does anyone ever know where he is?" He walked away from the girls and went to talk to Don Rodrigo.

"Let's run to his house and see if he's there, Mercedes."

They came upon Lucía and asked her where her son was, but she just shook her head and said nothing.

"Perhaps Antonio does not want to say goodbye," said Mercedes as they walked along. "Most boys don't, you know."

Teresa ignored her remarks. She did not want to leave without saying goodbye to Antonio, so she hurried ahead to his house.

"Wait for me," called Mercedes, trying to catch up with her friend.

"Antonio!" she called when they approached the house.

No one answered, so she pushed the door open to see if he was hiding inside. The house was empty.

"Where do you suppose he is?" asked Mercedes.

"Come, let's go," said Teresa. "I think you are right after all."

When they returned, the family had gone to the coach, and the peasants stood around talking to Don Rodrigo.

"Look, Teresa," cried Mercedes as the peasants stepped aside to let them go through, "isn't that Antonio sitting up in front next to Filimón?"

At the sight of them, Antonio stood up waving his arms and shouting, "Hurry, hurry, Filimón is waiting for you so we can go."

"We? To hear you talk one would think you were going along, too," said Teresa. "We have been to your house looking for you. Mercedes thought you did not want to say goodbye to us."

They climbed to their seats, expecting Antonio to jump down and join the group of peasants. But when Don Rodrigo motioned to Filimón and the coach began to move, they realized the truth of his statement. He was actually going to San Juan with the family.

The peasants cleared the way to let the coach turn, and Antonio looked at them over Filimón's shoulders.

"*Adiós, Mamá*," he called.

Lucía waved back at her son. It was the beginning of her dream for him, which, thanks to Doña Anita, had now become a reality.

"Why didn't you tell us about Antonio before?" asked Teresa.

"This summer was full of surprises," answered her mother. "You and Mercedes had one for Ramón and Lucio one for us all. This was mine for you girls."

"Not even Antonio heard of it until a few minutes ago," explained Grandmother. "I don't know who was more surprised, you or him."

When the coach turned, the peasants went running down to the edge of the path.

"¡*Adiós* Don Rodrigo!" they called, wishing the family good luck and a quick return.

"*Adiós*—farewell," came the answer from those in the coach.

Further down the road, Esteban and his family were waving. Antonio hung out of the coach in his eagerness to say goodbye to his friend.

The coach came out into the main road, and as they looked back they saw Ramón standing on the hill, surrounded by the workers. He stood there waving until the sight of the coach was lost upon the road, then turned and walked slowly back to the house. As he approached Grandmother's garden, he noticed the spot where Lucía had been working. The newly turned earth looked rich and black. He stopped to take a handful of it and held it tightly in his hand. It felt warm and moist. Suddenly, a feeling of loneliness came over him. He was alone for the first time since he had come to the *finca*. How would it be to live without the only family he had ever known? But was he really alone, when he had all the *finca* to himself and the peasants to do his bidding? And, finally, perhaps a reunion with his parents would reward his search when he looked for them in Guayama. Then he would have two families!

He let the earth slip through his fingers. "Good earth," he said softly under his breath. "I am your master now." Then squaring his shoulders, as he had often seen Don Rodrigo do, he gave the group of workers surrounding him his first order: *"Vamos, hombres*, let's go, men, there is work to do."

Recovering the U.S. Hispanic Literary Heritage is a national project to locate, identify, preserve and make accessible the literary contributions of U.S. Hispanics from colonial times through 1960 in what today comprises the fifty states of the Union.

Spanish travelers early on documented their journeys of exploration through the North American continent. Since then, Mexicans, Puerto Ricans, Cubans and others of Hispanic origin have also recounted their personal stories, passed on their lore and traditions, given creative expression to their novels, poetry, plays and other genres inherent to Hispanic traditions. As a result of this project, hundreds of thousands of literary pieces, including essays, autobiographies, diaries and letters will become accessible to scholars, students and the world at large. The publication of *Firefly Summer* is an early product of that research effort.

Recovering the U.S. Hispanic Literary Heritage will have immediate and long-term impact on the teaching of language arts, literature and history at every level of the curriculum. The emergence of this recovered literature will broaden and enrich the curriculum across the humanities, from the study of the Spanish language to the way we view history. Accessibility to and study of this literature will not only convey more accurately the creative life of U.S. Hispanics, but will also shed new light on the intellectual vigor and traditional values that have characterized Hispanics from the earliest moments of this country's making through contemporary times.